The 10 Ranch

To Ashley

♡

The 10 Ranch

A Glimpse Into The Old West

TERESA LANGLEY

Xulon Press
555 Winderley Pl, Suite 225
Maitland, FL 32751
407.339.4217
www.xulonpress.com

Paperback ISBN-13: 978-1-66288-465-8
Ebook ISBN-13: 978-1-66288-466-5

THANKS, AND ACKNOWLEDGMENT

To my editor Wyatt Henson for his encouragement and support. Thank you for your assistance and all your hard work.

Chapter 1

Old, New, beginnings

Cat Avery sat on a large slab of limestone. The reigns of her horse on the ground beside her. She loved the flint hills. The tall grass was waving with the breeze. Her 16th birthday was just two days ago. Feeling melancholic after her brother's recent departure, she couldn't help but reminisce about the beginning of "The 10".

Her grandparents had "The 10", a ranch they settled in the Flint hills; The month after they were married. She had very little memory of her grandparents Howard and Eva Webb. They had two children, a son Joe and a daughter May. Their daughter was Cat and Colton's mother. She had no memory of them at all; Joe married Suzzane and remained on the 10 after they married. Joe and Suzzane were never able to have children of their own but raised Cat and her twin brother Colton as their own.

Almost sixteen years ago Howard and his wife were eagerly awaiting the arrival of their daughter May and her husband Charles. May and Charles had made their home in Springfield soon after they were married. May had been gone with Charles for almost a year.

Pappy, a young ranch hand at the time, opened the door to the house and called in "Riders are coming from the gate" Howard looked up "It's a covered wagon"

Howard, Eva, Joe, and Suzzane left the house and waited in the lane. Along with the covered wagon, another man then rode his horse along with them. The wagon pulled to a stop in the lane outside of the house. The rider stepped off his horse and asked "Which of you would be Howard?".

"I am" Howard stepped forward, the confusion being clear on his face. "And you are?"

"The name is Garret sir" he glanced at the wagon. "We can talk later, for now, these folks both need a hand down"

Joe, Howard, and Garret helped the man down "Pappy" Howard hollered out "We'll be needing hands".

"Charles, is it really you?" Eva said a bit of panic in her voice.

"Hello, Mother Webb." He replied in a weak voice.

"Where is May?" she said in a curious tone

"She is in the back resting."

After a bit, and with the help of two more ranch hands, Charles and May were inside the big house. Both were put to bed in separate rooms for some much-needed rest.

Howard asked Garret to join him in the kitchen, the coffee was ready.

As Cat recalled the story, Garret had met up with her parents covered wagon along the road. He had been riding in the same direction as they were. He was out looking for work.

Her parents had stopped to rest for a full day when Garret had ridden up on them. May was very pregnant and looking rather worn out.

Charles offered him coffee which he gladly accepted. He sat and visited with them for a while, taking the coffee and bread they offered him. During their meal, Garret had told them he was headed west to look for work, he was hoping to be a cattle hand. Charles told him he was ill and needed to get his wife May home to her folks; and that the babies would be coming soon. He asked Garret if he would help them and offered him decent pay.

"I'll help you out friend," he told them. "But I won't take any payment, I'm heading that direction anyways and maybe The 10 could use another hand. The chance to enquire sir will be paid enough"

An agreement was reached. Garret helped them break camp, then hooked up the team. They were five days out.

Sitting at possibly the biggest table Garret had ever seen. He saw Eva pour coffee into five cups.

"I would like to speak to your men-folk mam, if you'll beg my pardon" Garret forwardly put.

Mrs. Webb grinned. "Young man" she replied softly "This is 'The 10' and there are no secrets in our home. No offense to you, and I take none from you. Things run better when everyone knows what is going on"

"Yes mam", Garret smiled "My parents are like this, but few I've met rarely are. I will speak openly." Turning to Howard he continued. "Charles has cancer. He is a very sick man; He isn't contagious but the doctors said they cannot help him."

Unshed tears filled Suzzanes' eyes "Her letters never told us any of that." Her voice traveled off "And help with the twins coming."

"Yes, mam" Garret replied, "he is hell-bent, oh excuse my language, ladies, on getting Miss May home, so she's not alone raising those two."

Chapter 2

BITTER SWEET TRUTHS

Looking out over the tall grass Cat stretched and daydreamed about the story, she figured it would be better to be heading in. She thought she'd join the ranch hands as they rode to the big house.

Cat referred to all the men on The 10 as "the boys". She was rather quick-witted which had to be due to her smaller stature, coming up to only 5'2" everyone on the 10 towered over her. Including her Aunt Suzzane.

Standing on her saddle she could see four of the boys gathered together. One waved his hat at her as she approached them. She kicked her mount into a slow lope.

"Been out scouting, all around today kitty cat?" Pappy was trying to start a conversation with her, but she didn't reply.

"It's been two days Cat," Garret said "Ya can't stay mad at Colt forever... he'll be back"

Cat swatted her horse into a slow trot the boys beside her stated. "I can't tell none of ya what I'm thinking about Colt... or I'd have to wash my mouth out with soap", while they rode up back to the house.

Suzzane had been like a mother to her entire life. She had a close friend she called mother. Her aunt didn't want Cat or Colton to call her mom or mother or anything except Aunt. She had told them many times that she was proud to be their aunt, and she had raised them like they were her own.

When Cat went to bed that night she cried quietly. Cat refuses to let anyone see her cry. She didn't often talk to God but believed in Him. Before Aunt Suzzane passed, they would go to church, here on the 10. They had built a small church and the preacher came once a month. That night .... something stirred Cat to talk to God.

Cat spoke quietly into the darkness.

"God, my mom died when Colt and I were three days old. I didn't know her, but everyone says that she was a good woman. My dad passed when we were six weeks. Next, God, you took Aunt Suzzane when Colt and I were 10. Please, God, watch out for Colt, please don't take him away from me too. Cause you know everything; you know he left to go scout for the Calvary in the army. He is a knothead for heading out. My heart hurts, and I feel empty. Keep him safe, and now god... amen". Deciding to turn it over to Him, Cat had drifted off to sleep.

The next day one of the boys had the wagon ready to head out to the village with trade goods. A small band of Indians lived on the 10 so they would trade goods with them. They all got along and grew to need one another. Cat had always looked forward to this day, it was exhilarating. Tom had driven the wagon there. Cat and Randy were on their horses. Uncle Joe stepped out of the house "I'm not going today cat" He told her "You've done this for us many times. Don't forget

Daisy's herbs. See ya when ya get back." And with that, he headed back to the house.

When they arrived at the village Cat tied her horse to the wagon and headed to the center, carrying blankets, utensils, and headgear for the horses. The boys had brought the rest alongside her.

Washee, the holy woman greeted her "small one... I am here." The woman waved her to come over.

Cat greeted her friend "Good to see you Washee!" She sat her bundles down. Then she searched for something special. "I have a gift for you Washee..." Cat handed her a burgundy-colored bundle "I made this for you with my hands. It is not for trade."

Washee untied the bundle. She shook it out and examined it closely. "What is this strange blanket small one?" Washee was confused but pleased.

"It is called a cape my friend," Cat answered and then took it from her. "Let me show you Washee." Cat then placed the cape around her friend's shoulders and buttoned the three large brown buttons. "This will keep you warm when the snow falls. You won't have to hold it, and it won't fall off. Also, look it has pockets so you can take your trinkets with you, or keep your hands warm inside them. Pockets are great!"

"You bless me small one" Washee's smile radiates a great amount of happiness and thanks. "And my dear child I have made you a gift as well" Washee handed Cat a pair of Moccasins. But these were nothing like Cat had ever seen. Quickly she sat down in the dirt and pulled off her boots to try them on. They were made like boots, but the tops came to the bend behind her knees. "I love them Washee! They are much more comfortable than these boy boots. A wonderful gift!" Cat hugged Washee. Washee was one of the Indian elders. She and Cat had grown very close over the years.,

"Washee could you please see to it that Keoto gets these old boots of mine?" Cat smiled "I won't be needing them anymore." Her feet felt like they were standing on clouds.

The holy woman took Cat's hand and leaned in to look into her eyes," The great spirit hears you small one. Your heart needs to know this. Colt will be cared for. Colt will return to you"

"But... But how do you know this?" Cat's voice was a faint whisper. "I talked to God but just last night."

"Small one," Washee tapped her forehead with her finger "The great spirit is with me at all times, he shows me things, he tells me." The woman tapped Cat's chest "He hears you and wants you to know, Colt will be safe." Washee stroked Cat's hair "Now you must live to know this in your heart, and forgive your brother, just let your anger for him pass. Breathe now child and go... go" She shooed Cat away.

That evening after their meal back at the big house the kitchen was buzzing. Randy and Tom helped Cat and Daisy clean up the mess from the meal.

"Good to see yer back with us Cat, I'm guessing you've forgiven Colt for high tailing it?" Randy teased.

Cat doused him with soapy water and Tom was caught in the crossfire.

"Now you've done it Kitty Cat!" Tom picked her up and headed out the door. Randy was right behind him pulling off Cat's new moccasins as they went. The two of them threw her in the horse tank. Water splashing and spilling everywhere.

Before they could even blink Cat splashed them back. "This is war", she screamed. The yard was filled with all the boys and everyone was laughing, splashing, and having a good time. Even Uncle Joe and Daisy joined in.

Chapter 3

HOUSE RULES

Daisy was an Irish woman that Aunt Suzzane had hired on to help her feed sixteen hard-working ranch hands. She lived in the big house in a room of her own. Everyone loved her but Daisy had her own rules and expected everyone to live by them, including her boss, Joe Webb.

Every day Daisy swept and mopped the floors. The men that stomped through the house leaving dirt, mud, or barnyard debris would quickly meet Daisy's Irish temper. To her, it wasn't considered acceptable behavior. Every meal in the big house was served at the big table. But, before any of the boys could eat, even Uncle Joe, they had to leave their shoes on the porch. Cat's new moccasins would be fine though, as they were very clean.

They were soft-soled and didn't make much of a mess.

Cat helped Daisy prepare the early meal, she then excused herself before the boys came in. She told Uncle Joe she'd only be a minute. Quickly she ran out the back door.

"What's that wee child up to now Joe?" Daisy asked.

"Well," Joe replied. "It's Cat, it could be anything..." They both laughed and chuckled about it.

Cat was at the table before the boys missed her. The chatter was light and fun. They discussed what would be done for the day. Uncle Joe wanted Cat to get a calf count for him with Garret's help.

It was Pappy and Joe's turn to help with the mess of the dishes and the kitchen. Cat and the boys headed out the door. The boys had to stop on the porch to pull their boots as Cat headed straight for her horse already saddled.

"Ouch... Ouch!" Randy yelled out. It was too late

"Dang yer hide Cat!" Tom screamed they were on the ground trying to get their boots off.

Uncle Joe, Daisy, and Pappy were laughing. "Guess Cats over pouting about Colt leaving" Joe smiled. "She is back to pulling pranks on the boys."

"Yep" Pappy agreed, "The boys sorta' started it with the bath in the tank last night"

"Aye," Daisy chimed in "That wee one can sure even the score though" They all laughed.

Chapter 4

Unexpected Visitors

As the years rolled on, Cat adjusted to her twin's absence. The emptiness in her heart remained. When the boys would reminisce about him, she couldn't contribute to the conversation. They noticed but thought it was good for her to hear about the good times when he was home. A letter would come a few times a year and she would listen as Uncle Joe read it, usually at a meal.

The last letter they received told them that he would be home soon. "Soon", Cat said mockingly "Soon, but not when.... not even a maybe this day...... or that week.... he is such a brat." Out the door, she went.

She was racked with emotion, but happy he was at last coming home. Sad because she didn't know when, mad because he'd left in the first place. Guilty for being upset with him at all. It was what he wanted to do... so he had just up and done it. She missed him so much.

Cat had taken supplies to the bunk houses on the 10. The first two went to the SE and then the SW Bunk houses. There were two sacks for each house. They contained meat, potatoes, dried fruit, bread, paper, pencils, ink, along with a few other items. The sacks would hold the boys who rode the cattle and stayed in those bunkhouses for two weeks. Two in one day was quite the ride because of the distance and back from the main house. She chose the South first because they were the closest.

The next day Cat loaded her horse with the sacks for the NE bunkhouse and headed out. The distance would only let her travel to that one today.

When she reached the NE bunkhouse, she pushed the door open. She walked to the trap door and dropped the sacks on the table down below and to the side. One bunkhouse to go.

Patting her horse on his neck, and stepping back onto the saddle, she headed out.

The next day as she headed for her last stop she kept her eyes and ears on high alert. The warning from Keoto was fresh in her thoughts. She couldn't be at ease knowing someone had been around.

She had spent several days out riding the 10 checking for signs, tracking, and backtracking two unknown riders.

"Settle down Cat" she spoke out loud to herself. "Stay alert but relax a little"

Coming up on the last bunkhouse, nothing seemed out of order.

Cat slowly loped her horse up the lane and stopped it at the hitching post outside the northwest bunk house. He dipped his nose in the water tank for a cool drink and quickly brought it up, ears pricked back and staring into the distance quietly blowing.

"Don't start looking for the boogieman, I'm already jumpy enough as it is." Reaching behind her saddle, she gave the string a quick jerk and released the tie on her pack. Hopping off her horse she slid the two bags tied together like a makeshift saddle bag onto her shoulder.

Turning toward the bunkhouse she patted her horse's neck and whispered "This is our last supply delivery for two weeks. She knew the house was empty with all the men still counting cattle and calves, readying for the round-up later in the month.

Quietly climbing the steps, she reached up and swung the door open. Cat froze in her tracks; the bags fell to the porch floor. The next few seconds seemed to come together in slow motion... without realizing it her right hand was already drawing her trusty revolving pistol. A large hand grabbed her right wrist before she could even take her gun out of the sheathing. Her left arm was captured and pulled tightly against her side as she was lifted off her feet. Her back crushed against a large solid chest. Fear swept through her. In the next instant, the warm breath of a man whispered in her ear....

"Good morning sis."

Her grip loosened; Cat jerked herself around clambering out of his arms her brother still holding her pistol by one finger.

"Did you lose something, Sis?" He had the biggest cocky grin spread across his face.

"Damn you Colt" She gasped and threw herself into his arms knocking him backward off the porch.

"OOF" was the sound he made as she practically knocked the wind out of him.

"Oh my god Colt, I've missed you so much." Total joy spreads across her face. They picked themselves off the ground and dusted off a little. Colt motioned her to go into the house with him. As Cat stepped onto the porch with her brother behind her, still laughing she suddenly turned around and punched him in the chest. It was hard, enough to cause him to stumble back a few steps.

"I could have shot you sneaking up behind me like that you're a dumbass!" Cat yelled.

"Hey, hey, hey now, language. Geez Cat, still quite the potty mouth I see" Colt Chuckled.

Cat took another swing at him and he picked her up, he kept her fists pinned together heading into the bunkhouse. They were laughing all the way when Cat suddenly remembered the man she forgot was standing at the door when she originally was going for her gun. The same man she laid eyes on when she opened the door. This man was wearing only his jeans and was barefoot. Reaching for a cup, he poured her some coffee and set the cup before her. Colton piled her into the empty chair as the three of them caught their breath. Colton picked up his coffee and leaned over the table looking her in the eye and stated.

"What seems to be the emergency, Sis?" as he tapped the paper wire gram laying there. His eyes showed concern and as always, he got straight to the point.

Jumping up from the chair, Cat went to the old small desk in the corner. She opened the top drawer and pulled out a sheet of fresh paper, took a short pencil from the cup on the top, and returned to the table.

She laid it in the center of the table and then took a sip of coffee. Surprise and delight flashed across her face and danced into her eyes.

"Damn Colt this is amazing..." She took another sip.

"Cat! Your mouth, geez." Colten warned.

"Oh yeah, whatever..." She waved her hand around in the air.

The stranger was sitting back in his chair enjoying this 5 ft 2, petite little spitfire besting his 6 ft 2 friend. She was stunning.

"Okay," Cat began tapping the blank paper.

"This" She indicated "Is our property, the entire 10." Taking her pencil, she placed an "x" a little down and inside each corner of the sheet. Went to each of the "x" and put the appropriate bunkhouses in the corners and then drew a small circle where the Indian village was. She went closer to the center and drew six small squares clumped together and said "The homestead, headquarters"

Laying her pencil down she sat back in her chair as Colton started to speak, she held up hers and said with a spark of fear in her eyes "Please Colt hear me out."

Tension seemed to slowly drift off and away from her. She seemed to relax just a little. She took another sip of coffee, murmured a very vocal "mmm" swallowed, and began.

"Seven days ago, Keota came to me at the big barn with a message from his grandfather." Cat Stated.

"Whose Keota?" the stranger asked.

"Atokee's son, they have a village here on the 10" Colton answered him.

"Keota said on two different days, hunters from their village had come across two riders. The hunters stayed hidden and watched these riders slowly scout around. These riders themselves tried to stay hidden" Cat had their full attention.

"I went to the house and left a note for Pappy so he would know what I was up to. Uncle Joe was gone to Coffeeville during this time and I needed to tell someone where I was going." Cat took another drink of coffee and moaned aloud again. As she sat her cup back down it seemed to magically fill back up again.

"Damn it Cat" Colton started.

Cat threw her hand up in the air and exclaimed "Oh my what a potty mouth!" mocking her twin with a touch of ornery dancing through her eyes.

"Shut up and let me finish" Cat stated with clenched teeth.

"Colt, for four days I scouted and scouted and backtracked those two riders. I had never seen them, not once, but I had found everywhere they had been.

"Mam" the stranger stated as he stood up.

Forgetting that he was there, Cat stood up.

"Oh... hey, where are my manners?" Colt jumped up to his feet saying. "Let me introduce you two." He began. "Cat Avery" both of his hands at waist height tipped towards his twin, holding the same gesture and turning to the stranger and stating, "Matthew Webster."

Matthew extended his hand, Cat extended hers and they both said "Nice to meet ya" as they shook hands with each other.

Matthew asks Colt "Are you thinking maybe rustlers?"

"That could be what this is, the cattle drive is coming at the end of the month. Right Cat?" answered Colten.

"Colt" she growled, "let me finish... please." Cat's face was sincere almost pleading for them to hear her out.

"Ok, sis... I see you seem a little stressed, please, I'm sorry... continue." Colt sat back down.

"Now as I was saying, I don't think it's rustlers. That was what I suspected at first. However, they never approached the livestock... ever." She went on to tell them all about the bunkhouses that had been watched. She had even found where the main house had been watched as well. The riders had stayed low in the gulley and washes to keep themselves hidden.

Cat looked over at Colton and realized he had a very amused look on his face.

She could feel her anger begin to boil. "What Colt.... why are you smirking at me? This isn't funny to me at all!"

Colt relayed his smirk and slowly moved his eyes down her arm, stopped, then back to her eyes. Cat turned her eyes to see what he had

looked at. She felt the blush burning her cheeks.
She had stood there talking to them for well over
five minutes and had never released Matthew's
hand after the handshake. She was still holding
his hand, and Matthew seemed to be pretty
happy about it.

With Colton laughing, and Matthew not
making a sound, Cat jerked her hand back to her
face, then turned on Colton again. But this time
her passion was a little defeated. She simply muttered, "Colt, You... Are... A Jerk sometimes."

Matthew divided the rest of the coffee
between the three of them and Cat practically
dove into hers. Again, she sipped and moaned
"This is so good colt, how did you make this
amazing coffee"

Smiling, Colton pointed to Matthew.
"Wasn't me sis, it was him."

Cat gave Matthew a slight nod and lifted her
cup. Sort of like a toast.

As Colton turned to his sister, he began to
spill his thoughts as to why he thought that they
might have been rustlers. As he droned on about
the old man Jackson and when they ran off some

cattle rustlers' years ago. Matthew, still wearing only jeans, laced his fingers behind his neck and rocked his chair back onto two legs.

Cat looked up at the Ceiling and thought "Here we go, I'm exhausted and he is going to start rambling on and on."

Out of the corner of her eye, something caught Cat's eye. Still looking up she tilted her head slightly and watched it. Closing out her brothers rambling and blabbing.

Ever so slowly, her eyes dropped to the tiny creature that seemed to magically stop in mid-air. Then it quickly dropped.

Before Cat realized what she was doing, she vaulted over the edge of the table and whacked Matthew upside the neck. The two of them tumbled to the floor. Matthew was still seated in the chair, flat on his back with Cat on top of his shirtless chest. Cat's hand still clamped on his neck. Colton jumped to his feet.

After the crash, you could have cut through the silence with a knife.

Then, "Cat!" Colt yelled. "Have you lost your ever-loving mind?"

Her eyes locked with Matthew's eyes; she was still lying on top of his naked chest. She smiled with the biggest smile ever and simply said. "A spider fell on his neck." With her elbows still on his shoulder she rolled her hand palm up. Sitting in the center of the palm of her hand was a very squashed spider. At the same time, Matthew and Cat erupted into some hysterical laughter. A few seconds later, Colton was doubled over the table holding his sides and laughing alongside them. After what seemed like an eternity of laughing. Cat caught Matthew's eye and winked at him, then whispered "Help me get up", with a sheepish grin, "Then you can watch me get even with him for scaring the crap out of me."

With an easy and gentle movement, Matthew lifted Cat up and over himself while still flat on his back on the floor. He then stood himself straight up beside her. He stood a full foot taller than Cat. She looked him square in the eye and gave him a smile that made her eyes sparkle with pure mischief. With her palm still up holding a dead spider she chased her brother around the room. Colton screamed like a small girl.

The dead spider soon fell from her hand. Then Colton turned the chase around, heading towards Cat. She bolted towards Matthew, "Save me, save me, I give up!" Cat laughed. As she reached Matthew's side, he grabbed her and slipped her around behind him to playfully protect her from her twin.

"You're cheating Cat!" He gasped still laughing. "Matthew is bigger than I am." The laughter quieted down, the three of them still smiling. Matthew pulled Cat carefully around in front of him.

Suddenly Colton's body jerked forward hard as he crumpled to the floor. That's when Matthew and Cat heard the shot that ripped through her brother's body.

With one arm Matthew slammed Cat's back hard into his chest grabbing his gun belt off her chair as they went down. He quickly rolled her off of him to his left and noticed she already had her gun drawn and ready.

They lay there both with a window beside them. Matthew Cocked his head to the side. He put his finger to his lips asking for her silence. She nodded slightly. They could hear a horse running fast and hard, trying to distance itself from the house. They lay there for a few seconds, for what had felt like an hour. Matthew said, "They are gone."

Colton moaned; Cat was at his side in an instant. It took Matthew a few seconds to pull on his boots and shirt. Cat screamed "Get the horses, I'll try to stop the bleeding"

Colton had been in the barn saddling up when Cat had ridden in that morning. Matthew was making coffee. The horses were ready so Matthew hurried inside. As he charged in the door, he was afraid of how he might find Cat with what had just happened. She was calm and collected, very much in control.

"Matthew," she said sternly. "The bullet went right through. I don't think that it hit anything crucial. However, he is losing way too much blood. Grab me the kitchen towel!" Matthew quickly handed her the towel. She pulled out the knife that was in her boot to cut the towel into wide strips. Doing her best, as fast as she could, she would wrap his wounds. Colton's head had a nasty open gash from the corner of his eye to his eyebrow. Shocked at how she only now noticed, she glanced over to Matthew with concern in her eyes. Her eyes holding a question her lips couldn't manage to utter. Afraid about losing her composure Matthew tells her "There was only one shot fired Cat. He hit his head on the table corner as he went down. Hold it together, we need to get him to those who can help him!"

Huffing a few breaths in and out she nodded then spoke. "Let's go, get him on his horse."

Matthew didn't need Cat's help. He simply lifted and rolled Colton into his saddle. Cat was already mounted when Matthew swung into his. Colton started to open his eyes, they flickered slowly.

"Cat" Matthew called gently. "Snug up to his left, and I'll stay on his right. Cat, you need to lead us out. I don't know where we are going."

When Colton was awake, he would hold his own, then and again he would succumb to the darkness. It took the both of them to keep him in the saddle. Matthew watched Cat as they traveled in silence. She kept them hidden in the washes, gulleys, and lower places as much as possible. Cat's steady pace was impressive, her eyes watching her surrounding constantly. Well over an hour had passed since they'd left the bunkhouse.

Cat pulled up to a stop and turned to face Matthew. She took a drink from her canteen and looked at her brother's saddle horn, then Matthews. Before she could ask Matthew said "They were filled and ready. We left them on the sideboard at the bunkhouse."

She handed him what was left of hers. Her eyes looked at his and she said "We are close. When we top that ridge, you'll see the homestead about two miles straight ahead. You'll be past all the washes and gulleys. He's lost a lot of blood and I'm pretty scared about that. I'm going to leave you. I'll bring help. Keep him safe, yourself too!" She turned and said, "Let's go!"

As soon as the three of them topped the ridge, Cat took off like a streak of lightning. She and her horse were in perfect sync. There, about two miles away, he could see the homestead come to view.

Matthew continued forward at a slow pace holding Colton in his saddle. His eyes watched in amazement as Cats horse stretched with ease at the fast pace, she was pushing him. He returned to his focus on the task at hand.

Cat's horse, at breakneck speed, pounded up the lane. She knew during the heat of the day more than half the boys would be at the barn. Noting Pappy and Garret standing up from their chairs on the bunkhouse porch as she passed them, turning her horse towards the barn. Pappy was screaming at her "You trying to kill your horse?!"

Pulling hard on the reigns her mount was sliding up to a stop, dust flying. Cat's feet were on the ground before the horse had fully stopped. The horse was fully lathered up head to toe drenched in sweat.

"I need four riders now!" She frantically screamed. Uncle Joe was running to her from the house.

"Colt has been shot Garret!" she screamed. "Get on that wagon!"

She pointed to the buckboard standing already hitched up in the shade.

"You four backtrack me," Cat yelled at the boys, "it won't be hard" She commanded them.

The boys, ask no questions, nor stopped for anything, quickly mounted then speed past her.

By this time Uncle Joe had reached her,

"What do you need?" He spoke gently and steadily.

"At least four blankets and two canteens" She expressed rather concerned. They both ran to the house. While Joe grabbed up blankets, she filled the canteens and grabbed some extra towels from the kitchen. With the canteens slung over her shoulders, Cat tied the twine tightly around her towels. Out of the door she ran, Uncle Joe merely steps behind her as they jump onto their horses. Joe handed her the blankets, she held the bundles against herself as they turned out of the lane and quickly head for Colton and Matthew.

She quickly caught up with the wagon team and tossed the blankets into the back. Kicking her mount back up into speed as she passes the wagon and slowly catches up to the four ranch hands. They were trying to backtrack her trail with slight trouble. When they noticed her approaching, they moved their horses out of the way as she soars past them and followed her. At full speed, she blazes sitting low in her saddle.

Andrew commented as she flew past them and said "I've never in my entire life seen that kid look as scared as she was right now, we better keep up boys!" The four of them dug spurs in as they kicked their horses up to speed.

Cat and Randy were the first to reach Matthew. He was at a full stop, sliding down from his horse and holding onto a bloodied and pale-looking Colton.

Randy and Cat jumped down off their horses and helped Matthew lift Colton down from the horse.

"Lay his shoulders on my lap," Cat commanded as she sat down on the grass. The two men did exactly as she asked. Glancing at Randy "We don't need dirt in his wound." She snapped

Without a word Matthew cut and stripped Colton's shirt up and off him. Pulling the soaked towel away, Cat gently poured a little water onto a towel in her bundle, she dabbed off some dry blood and got the other four towels then started to dress the wound, two in the front and back securing a tight wrap on his pale body. Cat quickly tied the twine around her makeshift wrap. Her hands were covered with dry and fresh blood. Thinking to herself that this is all that she could do Cat let a shuttering sigh escape her lips. Matthew knelt beside her with Randy on the other side. The both of them held pressure on the wounds as Cat started to whisper to Colton softly. "Don't you give up now Colt, you hear me, brother?" Her voice was soft but reassuring and strong.

Matthew introduced himself to Randy as the other three caught up and dismounted from their horses. The wagon was almost there, and having a moment Randy introduced Matthew to the rest of them.

"This is Loren, that is Keith, and that gentleman is Andrew." Randy pointed to the boys accordingly, then pointed to Matthew. "This is Matthew, he is a friend of Colts."

Cat was struggling inside of herself to maintain control. She told herself that now is not the time to crumble in front of the boys. When she looked up into the eyes of Andrew, she saw shock and fear.

"Don't you dare look at him like that!" She turned her eyes to the wagon that pulled up to a stop. "He will be fine". Her thought simply tumbled from her lips.

"Toss me a blanket" Cat was handed one immediately and she spread it out over the grass. Randy and Matthew lifted Colton onto the blanket, and one man on each corner lifted him onto the wagon.

"Randy, get up there with him and make sure to keep steady pressure on the wound on his front, and back" Matthew took charge and Randy listening to the orders, shouts to Loren to get on his horse and follow.

Andrew climbing aboard says "I will keep him as steady as I can." Keith tied the two men's horses to the back of the wagon. Setting with the team in his hands Garret gave Cat a stern, dead stare. "You stay put until you get that animal cooled down or he won't make it back to the yard." He dared her to move or sass back. Clicking his cheek Garret slapped the reigns. The team of them took off to the house. All six wondered if they would make it back before Colton bled out.

Matthew stripped Cat's saddle free from her horse and dropped it into the ground. He spread her blanket over the horse, it was pacing a little, still blowing and heaving trying to cool down.

As Matthew turned to Cat, she was still, sitting on the blanket her brother had laid on, on her knees.

She was shaking from head to toe as tears streamed down her face. Matthew laying down on his side pulled her down beside him and held her gently. Brushing her messy hair back from her face, she snuggled her back against his chest and he whispered.

"He's going to make it Cat. Colt has lost a lot of blood, and he is weak yes... but nothing crucial was hit, the bullet went through cleanly."

Cat didn't reply. She lay there cuddling in Matthew's arms and began to relax. Not getting much sleep over the last eight days, she was exhausted.

Two hours later, Cat moved a little. She realized that the bare part of her arm was a little cool. She rolled over and snuggled into a wonderful warmth pulling her cold arm against the heat and sighing. A strong arm pulled her closer to the heat. Startled into a full awakening, she realized that she had only cuddled herself up into Matthew's arms. Slowly she lifted her sleepy eyes into a set of beautiful dark forest green eyes. Matthew Webster smiling down at her.

His warm body began to gently vibrate as he softly laughed. Cat met it with a smile, pulling away from him she sat up. The sun was soon to set over the horizon.

"What the he-..." she started but stopped herself "Heck" she finished. "I guess I fell asleep..." Jumping to her feet she muttered. "Uncle Joe is going to give me a tongue lashing when I get back... oh no... Colt." Panic had set across her face.

Taking her by the shoulder Matthew slammed her into his chest holding her arms pinned against her sides.

"Cat..." He said firmly. "Just stop... stop... shut that head of yours off for just a minute and listen to me." She felt stiff as a tree. Then slowly Cat began to relax. Slowly she laid her head against Matthew's chest and sighed deeply.

When she finally relaxed a little, Matthew pushed her away to arms-length, hands still resting on her shoulders. She missed his warmth already, but Matthew's eyes met hers.

"Garret rode up a few hours ago, he told me to let you sleep. He said that the doctor rode in as they made it to the house. Colt made it to his room, and the doctor is going to stay the night to make sure he was all right. Doc said he will make it; he just will take a little bit before his strength is regained. He praised you for tending to him the way you did. Didn't think there would be any infections. After his head was stitched up, they cleaned up the rest of him. Then he came around a little. Daisy force-fed him some beef broth out of her stew. Now he is resting." Cat chuckled.

"Daisy could force-feed a raging bull and there wouldn't be anything that the poor animal could do about it." She looked back into Matthew's eyes as though she was searching his warm embrace, snuggling hard against him. "Matthew Webster, I am freezing!" she said as she tried to snuggle even closer.

Matthew returned her hug and laughed. "Then we better head for home, besides," he added then turned Cat to face the north, "Isn't that storm clouds heading for us?"

"Oh shi-... shoot we better get a move on." Twice in one day, Cat put her potty mouth in check. With his back to her, Matthew grinned. She had already stolen his heart.

Chapter 5

Sparks Igniting

The next two days Matthew and Cat rode out around The 10 so he could get the lay of the land. At the beginning of the third day, all the boys were at the main house. Seated with their breakfast in front of them, chowing down. Nine pairs of boots lined the front porch.

"Hey Cat" Keith called out "Loren has a pair of dungarees he's outgrown, you want 'em fetched up here to try on?" Several of the boys chuckled. She looked at Matthew but she couldn't read his expression. Before she could answer, her Uncle Joe cut into the conversation.

"No, she doesn't." his words were laced with venom. "It's bad enough she'll only wear those ridiculous riding skirts. Which is only loose-fitting... floppy-legged britches as it is, at least they still look like a shorter version of a... I don't know... Kind of like a lady's skirt. So, throw those da... durn pants in the burn. I best not catch any of ya... what does she call yall... "boys?" yeah. That's what she calls ya, ever bring her men's pants to wear ya hear me?! Does every last one of you all got it?"

Almost in sync, they all responded "Yes sir, yes boss!" almost clambering over one another to say it.

"Now because I have everyone's attention, I have an announcement to make. I need two volunteers to ride out to the herd and tell the men 'All the men' they are to be here at dawn for breakfast tomorrow morning. We are going to have a meeting of sorts and it's da..." Joe glanced at Daisy. "Darned important. Not to miss."

Someone chimed in with "Oh they won't miss an invite to eat any meal of Daisy's, they will come."

Matthew watched all the rough-around edges cowboys pick up their plates and scrape anything left on their plates into the bucket, stack their plates on the counter top and head for their boots out on the porch. Matthew followed their lead, as he walked behind them to the door, Cat was smiling at him while she held the door. Matthew took a very quick look around, no one was watching and he planted a quick soft kiss right on her lips. He heard her catch her breath as he moved away and out the door. When he stepped through the door, he felt Cat's presence behind him. He stopped as he watched the men, all the men carefully checking the inside of their boots. Cat was quietly giggling behind him. He turned to her smiling.

"Why do I get the feeling that you are somehow the reason for this boot inspection that I am witnessing?" Matthew commented.

"Because she's a little spitfire." Tom relayed.

"An ornery little she Devil" Andrew chimed in.

"Too sly for her own good" Hunter shouted.

The rest of the boys had something equal in nature to comment about her. Some of them laugh, and others have a defeated sigh.

"Should I inspect my boots, babe?" Matthew inquired with raised eyebrows.

Then right in front of God and the boys, she grabbed his face with both hands and planted a soft passionate kiss right on his lips. Stepping back, she smiled and stated. "No honey, you are about the only one here that will never have to worry about your boots." With that, she turned and went into the house.

As Matthew turned towards the men, he could see they were as shocked as he was. Keith slapped him on the back and said "Buddy... you better grow some eyes in the back of yer head." They all roared in laughter as they headed out to meet the day.

Stunned by the kiss Matthew realized he was still standing there. Beside him, he heard Pappy say.

"I'll be darned. Never thought I'd see the day that any man could sweep our little kitty cat right off her feet." As he began his contagious laugh, he pulled Matthew's sleeve and said "Come on sonny, the boss wants us to talk a bit."

Colton was healing at a fast rate but was still weak. Matthew, Cat, Pappy, and Uncle Joe headed for his room. Daisy was on her way out the bedroom door with his empty breakfast plates. Everyone could hear Colton hollering after Daisy.

"Thanks, Daisy, for the real food this morning. It was great. Now if you would please just bring me my pants I'll get out of your way. Daisy... Did you hear me?"

With Garret joining them, the five flowed into his room. Colton was sitting up on the side of his bed with a sheet wrapped around him. It appeared he was in his birthday suit.

Uncle Joe replied "Yes, she heard you. I think the entire dad-blamed county heard you. No clothes. No Boots, not even a pair of socks until tomorrow. And Son, if you try it, I'm going to shoot you in the foot. Now... you got that or does it need say'n again?"

Knowing he was defeated Colton Sighed "No, I got it." Then just as quickly "But I could at least sit on the porch in the sun awhile!" Joe Webb glared him down. Colton threw his hand up. Subject closed it seemed.

"Down to business" Joe quipped. "Colt... the day after Cat got you home, she and Matthew

rode out around the 10. Cat showed him everything she learned and discovered. Yesterday,
Pappy, Matthew, and Cat discussed it. Listened
to her perception of it all."

Garret and Colt were at full attention. "By
afternoon the sheriff showed up with his infor-
mation, and here is what we've come up with…"

The discussion continued for hours. Plans
were laid out as well. We are preparing for the
gathering so…

All well-known neighbors having lived here
in the area for at least three years were invited to
bring their families. No exceptions and no one
new to the area should attend. All sheriffs and
marshals well known in the area were coming
with their families. They would bring a dish,
bread, or dessert of their choosing. Food, music,
and friendly companionship. Saturday at the end
of the month everything was set. All the local
Indian villages including those on the 10 were
coming in all, they were expecting around One
hundred and thirty souls.

Their meeting was over. All were in agreement Matthew and Cat stayed in Colton's room

as the rest of them left to finish their work. "Colt, you look so much better, but right now I can see you are tired," Cat said. "We are leavin' so you can rest. You have to get your strength; we have a lot we need you to do." Cat reached and took Matthew's hand to pull him out the door.

"Cat is right ya know. I don't know this land as you do. Nor the people coming in" Matthew replied.

"You are both right. I'm going to nap now... and Cat... You're holding Matthew's hand again." With that Colton Slept.

Without a word, Cat and Matthew headed to the barn. Matthew in the lead, when their mounts were ready, they stepped into the saddles.

"Where to?" Matthew asked

"To the big lake," She replied.

After the evening meal Cat, Matthew, and Randy helped Daisy out with the kitchen duties. Then Randy and Matthew headed for the Bunkhouse in the dark. Cat and Daisy prepared things for the morning meal. When they were finished Daisy handed Cat a pair of leather gloves. "Randy left his gloves; see to it that he gets them back. He's leaving before daybreak with Tom to do his morning checks." She also handed Cat a cloth sack with bread and fried bacon for the boys' early meal.

"Thank you dear, these bones aren't as young as they once were." Cat kissed Daisy on the forehead and headed out into the darkness.

As she approached the bunkhouse, she heard the friendly banter with the boys. She slowed her pace. Stopping just shy of its porch, Cat stopped to look up at the stars.

"Breathtaking" she mumbled with a smile across her face.

Before she had the chance to continue with Daisy's chore, Cat heard Garret.

"Matthew" He started "You've been here a while now so tell us what is your take on our wild kitty Cat?"

Cat froze in place. Matthew's answer was quick. "Lordy guys... Without a word, Colt had run out the back door. Pouring our coffee, I had just set the pot down when the front door came busting open. There stood the most beautiful woman I had ever seen in my life." Matthew's movement added drama as Cat watched through the window. Matthew acted it out. "She was going for her gun!" Matthew's face was still playing all the drama. All the boys were holding their sides cackling like hyenas.

Matthew continued "I had just fallen in love and now I was going to be shot!" The laughter raised the roof. Cat slapped her hand over her mouth to stifle her giggles. On her right Uncle Joe walked up beside her putting a finger across his lips and smiled. They stood quietly and listened, Joe hearing every word.

As Matthew continued to act out what had happened, he had the boys on the edge of their seats. "Colt grabbed her pistol and hand as he dead-locked her whole body back into him. Fear and anger flashed through those eyes of her and I just stood there I couldn't move." Laughter rang through the night.

"The next thing I knew the two of them were on the ground, rolling around in the dust, claws flying, Cat had him down." Matthew spurted out "She pounded him in the chest, knocking out his air! Suddenly it was over, she hugged him and they were back in the house having coffee."

"That's our Cat!" they all chimed in.

"Oh, but wait it's not over yet! We started talking business, then she drank some of my coffee."

Everything went deathly quiet inside the bunkhouse. Cat and Joe stood in the darkness waiting for Matthew's story to continue. Only Cat knew what was coming next. She reached over and placed Uncle Joe's arm around her shoulder.

"It must have been my great coffee," Matthew continued.

Loren and Hunter interrupted. "You best not let Daisy know we replaced her coffee out here. She'll skin us alive." Everyone nodded in agreement.

"Go on" Rob prodded. "Go on"

"Ok, it must have been my coffee but Cat seemed to be in a trance" His dramatization continued. "Her eyes seemed to be not focused on anything just drifting, sort of down. Here I am trying to impress her, ... All cocked back on my chair my hands resting on my head, just leaning back." Matthew leaped in the air. "Cat vaulted over the table straight for me." Matthew paused. "I was thinking man, I must be impressing her" Matthew jumped again. Every eye on him. "Then WACK" He slapped his neck with his hand. "She killed a spider right upside my neck." The guys rolled up in laughter. "Over went my chair flat on my back with Cat suddenly on top of the middle of my chest!"

Cat wondered if the neighbors could hear the laughing echoing throughout the county. Uncle Joe was holding his sides about to bust a gut.

"And then... and then." The bunkhouse was roaring as Matthew continued. "Cat chased Colt around the house with the dead spider still in her hand. Colt was screaming like a stricken rabbit."

Uncle Joe couldn't contain his laughter anymore. The bunkhouse door slipped open with the entire contents spilling out into the moonlight joining Joe as they laughed. With Cat still laughing, Matthew scooped her up into his arms bride style. Turning to face the men. Matthew claimed. "And that my friends when your little wild kitty Cat stole my heart.

With Pappy still laughing he smacked Matthew on his back and stated. "And you my friend... will never get it back" He glinted all-knowing warmth in his eyes.

Chapter 6

PASSIONATE FLAMES

Next morning before the sun broke over the horizon. Matthew had Colton out on the porch to watch it as the cool morning air barely moved.

"Oh, this is great Matthew... I was beginning to wither away in that room."

Cat could hear them hear them talking under the covered porch, just below her window. She lay there under the quilts warm and smiling at their voices. The next instant her heart was pounding in her chest.

"Colt" There was hesitation in Matthew's voice. "I haven't spoken to Joe Webb yet, I wanted to talk to you about it first." Matthew handed Colt a cup of his coffee.

"Is this your coffee Matthew?" Colton asked, and Matthew nodded and smiled. Cat heard Colton's question and flew out of bed jumping in her clothes as she went.

"Man, this is so good, if Daisy knew it would crush her." He sipped his coffee and relaxed breathing the fresh air and the view. Matthew hadn't said anything yet.

Cat, with a cup in hand, passed her uncle's office, the door was open. "Hold up," he said.

"ugh" is what Cat was thinking as she was on a mission. Uncle Joe stepped out in his socked feet, cup in hand, a grin on his face. He whispered to Cat. "I've heard these rumors and can't believe anyone's coffee could outdo Daisy's. So, I'm going with you!"

He pointed to his feet. Cat smiled and looped her arm through his. To the door, they went.

When the two of them reached the door arm in arm they froze in their tracks. With the door ajar, they heard Matthew's words. "I am head over heels in love with your sister. I can't get her out of my head/ I can't focus Colt. I can't wait to get up each morning and see her, smell her, touch her." Colton shot him a hard look. "No, now wait, Colt, it's not like that, I mean like touch her hand, for her to slide her arm into mind. You know me I would never disrespect her. I guess what I am asking for is your blessing... As I will ask Joe Webb for his blessing. Colt, I can't see living my life without her by my side.

"What if she turns you away?" was Colton's reply. "Cat is headstrong and extremely independent."

"Do I have your Blessings, Colt?" Matthew pressed.

Colton looked his friend in the eye, his face softened, then his smile grew wide. "You have it, my friend."

Joe Webb stepped out on the porch. Matthew and Colton got to their feet.

"I heard your words son. But... I need some coffee to ponder on whether you have my blessing or not" Matthew reached to the table beside him and grabbed the pot and Colton winked at him. As Matthew filled his cup Joe continued "Because I heard your conversation there's no reason to repeat them to me." Joe took a sip, and then another. He smiled. "You have my blessing, however... you might want to turn around and fill the other cup."

As Matthew turned around there was Cat, her cup hanging by a finger, tears streaking down her face. Matthew took her cup and handed it to Joe. "Babe... I didn't want this proposal to come to you like this. I had it all figured out..." Cat jumped into his arms; she was speechless.

Joe slapped him on the back and said "Well son, you just got handed your yes, however... you might want to fill her cup before she changes her mind." They all erupted with laughter.

As the four of them finished off the pot of coffee, Matthew and Cat headed hand in hand towards the bunkhouse leaving Joe and Colton sitting on the porch. Rob stood at the barn and yelled out "A rider coming in"

Matthew opened the bunkhouse door calling out "Cats coming in." Turning to Cat, he pulled her in by the hand and sat her down at the table. She looked around as Matt started making Coffee. Six of her boys were pulling on their boots for the day.

Each was grinning "At least we don't have to look for scorpions" another shouted "Or sharp rocks" a last one chimed in "Or horse turds." They all laughed, Cat giggled softly and looked at the table. No remorse.

Keith quickly turned the chair around; six men surrounded her. She blushed. "Kitty Cat are you not feeling well?" Said one "Down with a fever?" another asked. They all pretended concern. Finally, Hunter said in a true voice, "Ok Cat, what gives what are you up to?" No reply from Cat. "Ok guys, it's one of her booby traps. We best be looking out for it."

Cat looked at Matthew. He gave her a wink. Slowly she stood. Six men back up a few steps.

"It seems that Matthew Webster proposed marriage to me just a few minutes ago. I Cat Lynn Avery said yes!"

All six whooped and hollered. Picking up Cat, they hauled her over to the yard and took turns playing catch with her as she screamed at them that she was going to bust their chops.

Matthew stepped out. "The coffee is ready boys." Keith handed Cat to Matthew bride style and Matthew finally realized why Cat called them her boys. The two of them watched twelve men file one by one into the bunkhouse.

"You, my handsome man" Cat chirped "Are going to need to fix another pot." Then she kissed him.

After Matthew's 3rd fifteen-cup pot of coffee was ready. Cat climbed off his lap in the bunkhouse, Matthew picked up the pot and a fresh cup with Cat in tow they headed for the porch. As they stepped up Joe held the door.

"Shall we head for the table and get started?" He eyed the coffee as Matthew and Cat passed.

When everyone was seated Sheriff Martin nodded to Cat. "Now if you sweet lady will excuse us, we men would like to get started." His manners he thought made him look impressive.

"I think not sir.... I prefer to stay...., join in so to speak." Cat raised her eyebrows at him with a warm smile.

"Now you listen to me little lady" He began harshly. "This meeting is not for you to..." Matthew had him by the scruff of his shirt holding his vest, his feet dangling above the floor.

"How dare you speak to any woman like that!" Matthew growled in a very low voice. "Especially mine." Matthew's face was full of anger. His eyes were full of venom. Matthew slammed the sheriff's butt back down in his chair as fast as that happened. Dusting off his vest with the back of his hand. Matthew picked his hat up off his head and paced it in sheriff martin's lap. He turned and smiled at everyone else, with a wink for just Cat. He calmly sat down and spoke. "Now then if everyone will be seated again, we can start over. You okay with that babe?" Cat walked over and plopped down in Matthew's lap as he pulled his arms around her. Cat replied, "Yup thank you, sweetheart, is everyone ready to start again?" Sheriff Martin slowly stood. With shaky hands, he said, "I have two letters for Mr. Matthew Webster and a folder pouch for Joe Webb." Placed his hat on his head saying. "This concludes our meeting." Before he walked away from the table, he reached for the star pinned on his vest, pulled it off, and dropped it on the table. The shiny badge danced and spun.... then it settled and stopped.

The now Mr. Martin nodded and said "Good day gentlemen." He turned to the door, and Matthew cleared his throat before his second step fell. Mr. Martin stopped tipped his hat. "mam" and walked out the door.

Colton and Pappy burst into laughter. "Matthew... you made him piss his pants."

"What?" Joe thought Colton was joking. He looked to the floor there was a very large puddle. Joe clasped his hands over his head and shook it.

"Daisy is going to be so mad" Cat spoke softly. The room erupted.

"I'll get the rags out of the barn. I'd rather not have Daisy upset with me. Don't want her ruining that fancy mop." Matthew said as Cat followed him out the door.

Daisy entered the room with a plate of cookies just out of the oven. Her smile quickly faded. "Oh my."

"Now, now" Joe was on his feet, arm around Daisy's shoulders guiding her to the table "Matthew caused a little mess, he and Cat are on the way to the barn to fetch some rags." Pulling out a chair for her, he sat her down with the men. Pappy took a fresh cup and filled it with Matthew's coffee.

"Now then Daisy, you have some coffee with us and take yourself a break, those cookies smell really nice."

The men all grabbed a cookie as they sipped coffee, and watched carefully as Daisy took her 1st sip of the special brew.

"Wow..." The second sip going down. "This is like a wee pop of heaven." All the men released the breath that didn't even realize they were holding.

Everyone cleared out and fell into their daily routine as Joe pulled the reports from the folders and began to read. Early afternoon Garret stepped in the door to Joe's office "Riders coming in, looks like Steve." Joe looked up a smile spreading across his face. "It Figures, don't it, Joe." He smirked, humor dancing in his eyes.

"Call in Matthew, Cat, Colt, and Pappy... have Loren fetch Randy in. Tell Loren to take his place with Tom." Joe ran his hands through his hair and sighed.

Joe stood. "Wait... and Garret." Joe leaned across the desk "Spread the word, No one, I mean no one, is to be out and about alone. Everyone is to partner up. If someone finds themselves without a partner for rounds, they are to join up and go as three." Joe slammed his fist onto his desktop." Is this understood?"

"Yes sir!" But before Garret could reach the door.

"Wait." Garret turned. "Scratch that." Joe's mind was spinning faster than he could form words. Garret waited.

"Okay change of plans... send the men out in pairs of two... bring every hand in now... stay together as you gather the men... no one is to be left out. Get moving..."

"What are they like Matthew, how old are they, do you think..." Matthew halted Cat's questions with a kiss. She couldn't seem to get enough of his kisses. She couldn't remember being this happy. Breaking away from his kiss Cat said. "Look at what you've done, I'm so addicted to your kisses that's all I think about. You big brute." She playfully slugged him. "You big ole handsome wonderful brute. I love you so much..." Cat balled up her fist and screamed. "I don't want to wait any longer to become your wife!"

Laughing Matthew pulled her into his arms, calming her with a cuddle. "It's killing me too babe. It takes everything I have not to sneak into your window every night and get into your bed." Cat went calm, her blush burning her face. "You are so cute when you blush."

"Matthew what about the gathering?" Cat pulled away from him and an idea was already forming. She took Matthew's hand. She had his full attention. "Tom told me that the preacher is coming to the gathering. He and Bev, you know the girl, from Severy are going to be married that day."

"Are you sure babe, I know I am." Matthew said as he searched her eyes" From the second I laid eyes on you, and you didn't shoot me," he smiled "The look you shot me with those beautiful eyes went straight through my heart. I knew.... I knew that second. But I want you to be sure. I don't want you to feel like you are being pushed or rushed. Look at me Cat. Tell me what you feel."

Cat locked her eyes with Matthew's eyes as if boring through his soul. Then she said "That was the same day you told me I had stolen your heart. I.... I knew then. That I was already in love with you. You were the man that had somehow, someway melted away the ice that had closed off my heart. When Colt had ridden away.... we had just turned sixteen. I couldn't understand why he would do that. Now I know.... He probably didn't know then either...., I feel that God had sent him out into this world to find you. You this kind, understanding, wonderful, funny man, so he could bring you home to me."

They agreed to do it, that this is what they both wanted, one as much as the other. They would get married on the day of the gathering. It was then they heard the riders moving towards them.

"Matthew... Cat..." Randy called out. "Boss wants you both at the house... no one rides alone." Garret's voice rang true.

Cat and Matthew started leading their horses over to them. "We are on our way boys... see you there." Cat turned to Matthew. "Matthew

Webster, you are going to have to lean down here a little." She smiled slyly. "I'm too dang short to give you, my kisses." Laughing Matthew scooped her up bride-style into his arms. "Anytime babe... I promise you won't have to ask twice." After the requested kiss they were into their saddles and headed home.

The two of them put their horses out in the paddock after oats and a rub down. Joining hands as they walked to the house. Matthew bumped Cat's shoulder gently.

"We are adding a few more details to the gathering with our wedding. Would you like the honor of telling Uncle Joe babe, or are you wanting me to take this honor?"

Bumping him back, she smiled up to him and proudly said "Let's do it together."

Just over two hours later, sixteen hired hands, nine Indians, three family members, Matthew, Daisy, and the old, now the new Sheriff Steve, was all sitting at the big table. Thirty-one people in total. Chairs from the bunkhouse and off the front porch accommodated everyone. Laughing and chattering voices filled the house. It was about three o'clock in the afternoon.

Daisy had been cooking and baking all day. With her tasks complete Joe had asked her to join in. Saying that it would please him to have her accompany him. She mingled with them, all joining in chatter. When Pappy had told the men what happened that morning with the old sheriff, Daisy puts her fist against both hips, and with her very thick accent she boldly proclaimed "Had I'd known what happened on me floor, that lad would have knots upon his head put there by me, with me stick, then t'would have been him a cleaning his whiz up off me floor wit his own coat."

The men listening burst into laughter, knowing she would have done just that.

While the visiting was going on Cat took Matthew over to introduce him to the people of the village. The twelve-year-old Keota was her first introduction.

"Keota you now stand taller than me, look how you have grown," Cat told him.

"Miss Cat" Keota replied "Everyone will always grow taller than you." He was being sincere. "Even my baby sister will someday be taller than you. You are strong and brave, and you have a good soul, Miss Cat the great spirit has made you all good all over, but he didn't want you to be very big. You might be too big for him to control if he made you bigger. So be proud. Be strong also be understanding why he made you so small." He was finished with his opinion and she didn't know if she should smile or punch him. Matthew wrapped his big arms around her as he held his laughter. He nodded to Keota and spoke.

"You are very wise for your young age" Matthew received an elbow jab from Cat.

A small hand pulled her into a hug. "I have missed you, child." It was Washee. Tears pooled in Cat's eyes.

"Washee, I have missed you as well. Please I want you to meet the man that I will marry soon. Washee... this is my man. His name is Matthew Webster."

Matthew bowed.

"He gives me his love. He protects me and can hunt. We share anything and everything with one another."

"Sit... sit tall one. You are that of a great bear." Matthew sat on the footstool as Washee looked deep into his soul. She nodded keeping her old eyes on Matthews's eyes as if she was still studying him.

"Yes, small one; he has a good soul. It is very strong. He carries a burden that isn't his to carry. The great spirit gave him a task to do. He completed this task. The great spirit is happy... Satisfied. But your man does not understand about that..." Her gaze changed as she spoke directly to Matthew. "The great spirit wants you to understand, it needed to be done. No more suffering comes to any more people. The great spirit blesses you with life and happiness. With success and his protection."

"So now tall bear" Washee continues. She took two leather strings out of her pouch. Each string had one bead tied through it. "Take this binding and tie it around the small one's wrist." She watched Matthew as he did what was told.

It was tied. "Now small one" she looked towards Cat "Take this binding" she handed a binding to Cat. "Tie it around tall bear's wrist" Cat also did as she was told. It was tied. Washee placed the "Small one's" hand into the "Tall bear's" hand. "The great spirit now makes you as one. As the white man says, you are 'married', joined to each other. Go... go with my blessing too. She patted Matthew's cheek. As she walked away, she mumbled. "Nice to look at Cat"

"Well, now tall bear... small one. I am so glad we didn't miss the ceremony." Turning their heads in unison Uncle Joe and Colton were standing there, grinning from ear to ear. "It seems you are officially married. You may now kiss your bride." Colton finished smiling.

"Well then." Pappy and Garret were standing there too "This is good news, Matthew, get your stuff out of the bunk house and up to Cats room."

Pappy barked happily "We are going to need your bunk" Grinning as he walked away.

They both gave Garret a stunned look. "Aren't you going to kiss your bride?"

The entire room clapped and cheered. Everyone had been watching. Cat turned to Uncle Joe. Joe held his hands up and smiled again. "Keota came and told me what was getting ready to happen over here. I simply spread the word! Congratulations to both of you.

Matthew pulled Cat up into his arms and kissed her. Then whispered "Well so much for us adding more to his plate... the gathering!"

Cat smiled "I love you, Mr. Matthew Webster."

"And I love you Cat Lynn Webster," Matthew replied love stricken

"Ok... Ok... The fun is over, and the wedding and visit is over. Let's all take our seats and get down to business" Colton brought the meeting to order.

"So here we go. The locals haven't decided on a date for the cattle drive yet. They are close though and will notify us. Matthew, I don't know how much Colt has told you about how we operate that..." Joe Began.

"He's informed," Pappy spoke out.

"I'm thinking we'll know in about a week." Joe looked at his list. "Next... the local ladies including Washee" He nodded in her direction "have requested the 'trade' each month will start two days before the full moon, and through the day after." Joe drew a line through his second item. The entire room noticed his change in demeanor. "And now for the big item."

"As you know, two weeks ago Colt was shot." The room was very quiet. Joe ran his fingers through his hair. He seemed to pale. "That bullet was meant for Cat." No one said a word. But you could hear the room shift, to glance her way. Joe raised one hand. "It seems that maybe two months back, our little she Cat put a man in his place over at Sedan."

Cat stood up.... remembering.... Now her short fuse was suddenly on fire.

"The man was a fowl drunken pig." Cat was louder than she needed to be. "He put his hands on me, and I caved his face in with the butt end of my pistol. He was lucky I didn't shoot him."

Matthew pulled her down into his lap. There were a few chuckles and a few gasps Cat went silent. Guilt flooded her. Not for her busting that 'foul pigs' chops, but for her brother taking a bullet... meant for her. "I am so sorry Colt." She said touching his arm.

Pappy broke the silence. "If I recall the story... this was about the time that our little kitty Cat had just knocked Matthew flat on his back, and was back on her feet chasing Colt with a dead spider." Those who knew this story chuckled. Those who didn't sit wide-eyed, but also knew Cat.

"With that being said... the rest I will hand over to Steve... seems as if he is once again our sheriff." Joe took his seat. He added, "I want all of you to listen to him, and listen well."

Steve stood and then laid the folder pouch down on the end of the long table.

"It seems that the bullet meant for Cat pulls this area into a scandal that has spread across this country. This pouch contains the reports written by several Pinkerton agents. The report about Cat is only one of the many reports." All eyes were on Steve. All ears were listening.

"Joe and I have sat and read every report. We will add the report of Colt getting shot. His is a bit different from the rest. Because of the fuss this shooter and Cat had, we now know, that that man had been arrested in Sedan. He caused some problems while drinking too much later that same day. It was the same day that Cat way-laid him. While he was in his cell, he told another prisoner who he was. That he worked for the Tully company and that Cat was the same as dead." Steve paused.

"Now then.... even if this man had never laid eyes on Cat, the company he works for would still be part of the risk. It's the Tully company. This company runs across the territories looking at land for a railroad. When the company started, it was a legitimate establishment. A fair and generous man ran it. Yes, he made money doing this, but it served a purpose. That man died. His only son, a spoiled, mean man is now in control. Greed is his motive. The only reason this continues is that so far, the Pinkerton and local law hasn't been able to get hard evidence against him." Tipping his cup to show it was empty, his eyes went to Daisy.

Cat and Matthew were on their feet helping Daisy in a blink of an eye working on getting the three large pots returned and filling cups across the room as Steve continued.

Steve had asked Joe to take up the report from there. Matthew, Daisy, and Cat started making another three pots, it appeared as though it would be needed. They sat the extra pots on top of the wooden stove to keep it hot, returning to their seats and listening intently.

Matthew stopped Cat from taking her chair and pulled her into his lap. Cat leaned back against his chest and quietly sighed. She began to relax, Matthew's arms crossed around her waist.

Joe took all the reports out of the pouch and laid the stack on the tabletop. Picking up the top paper he looked at them and then laid them face down beside the rest. "The Tully company cheats and swindles folk out of their property. They first scout the land. Then they make a below-the-market offer. The landowners are sometimes found later dead. Others just disappear." Joe picked up the next report.

"Their tactics have gotten worse as they go. Several months back they have begun to kidnap folk, demand their land be sold for pennies on the dollar, only to have their loved ones... the Victims they kidnapped, to be returned. That is after the purchase was made." The room was deadly quiet.

The meeting went on for another half hour. When Joe and Steve finished speaking the room was open for questions. The warning was clear. Only a few questions were asked.

"Now" Joe continued as the room hushed a little. "All of you here today are like family to me, Colt, and Cat, and we've thrown Matthew into the pot as well." Colt smiled over at Matthew.

"Not one of you is to ever find yourself alone until this is over, ride in at least groups of two. I am not asking you... as part of my family... I am telling you." He then turned to the woman at his side "Daisy... if you need supplies .... you are to take three of the boys with you. You are not to be left alone here either... ever...." Joe was lovingly caressing Daisy's shoulder. The feelings he had been harboring for her all these years were clearly visible in his eyes. "Do you boys under-stand my meaning...? Sort it amongst yourselves. I trust everyone in here to abide by my wishes."

Joe turned to his left "Patoee, none of your braves, hunters, or squaws are to be alone. To you my friend I am not telling you, I am begging you to consider this." Patoee was the Chief of his people.

"All that live here on "The 10" need to be safe and aware at all times." Patoee smiled and bowed slightly. Joe stood to his feet. Clapped his hands. "With all that being said... Daisy and I have food and drinks ready, let's eat"

It was about 4:30 in the afternoon by the time they started to eat.

The meal was over before anyone had noticed. Hunter, Matthew, Cat, Joe, and Daisy cleaned the mess up from the kitchen. Daisy was unusually quiet. Cat knew with the men busy during the day, that Daisy was alone.... a lot. Then Cat remembered. "Matthew!" Her voice cracked out a little too loudly. The four in the room turned to her "Your sisters will be at the gate around Nine tomorrow." Next, she spoke to Hunter. "You'll need to send the buckboard and saddled horses for each of them. They prefer the saddle rather than the surrey."

Turning to Daisy now. "We need to clear out a few rooms and adjust for meals... oh sorry Daisy you know more about that than I do." Cat smiled.

She turned back to Hunter, she could see Matthew leaning on the sideboard, arms folded and across his chest... smiling "Also, you need the boys to help with the luggage and for their safety. Next..."

Hunter cut her off "Okay... Okay... slow down their kitty Cat. "Breathe..., Matthew... I'll take care of this. Around nine in the morning, you would say?"

"Yes, the stage will be coming in from Baxter Springs and I'm told their driver won't tolerate folks making him late." Matthew was still relaxed. As Hunter exited out of the kitchen door; Joe, Pappy, and Garret stepped in. All three were grinning ear to ear.

"Now cat" Uncle Joe hesitated then wrapped his arms around her for a hug. Releasing her, she stepped back still smiling.

"Most of the time, you are one step ahead of me and the boys. While you've all been in here lollygagging," Daisy swatted him with a towel.

"We've all got a wedding present for the two of you." Cat's face fell into shock. "So, Matthew, pick up your little lady... the way you always do, and bring her this way..." Happily, Matthew did just that. Daisy followed behind them.

Across the yard stood the original homestead house. four bedrooms, a large kitchen, and a dining area with a smaller sitting room. Cat had only been inside there a few times in her life. It had stood empty with its curtains drawn shut, for what seemed like forever. Pappy held the door open for Matthew as he carried his bride across the threshold.

"Now we aren't as good at cleaning and such as Daisy, but me and the boys done a pretty good job for you two." Garret smiled as he spoke.

Randy joined in "We swept and mopped..." Looking towards Daisy he continued." We sorta swiped yer mop gadget, Miss Daisy. Floors are clean." He puffed his chest out with pride.

Tom added "While they were doing that, me and Andrew took all the dust covers off the furniture and pictures. Then we wiped everything.

We've seen Miss Daisy do those things, so we did it as she does it."

Everyone commented then Keith gave his bit as well. "Loren, Bart, and I cleaned out the fireplace. This place hasn't got any pot belly but that fireplace works and it'll do you good."

The rest in turn told them what they had done to get the place ready. Uncle Joe was proud. Slipping his arm through Daisy's all of them turned and headed out the door.

"Stop right there Randy." Daisy stomped her foot. "Now where would me mop be found, young lad." Randy gulped. "I'll fetch it." Everyone howled with laughter as a visual shudder went through him.

Cat turned and put her face into Matthew's chest. She wrapped her arms around his waist. His arms enclosed her in a tender hug.

Cat's body began to shake as she cried softly. "Babe," Matthew said. "Are you, okay?" She wouldn't let him pull her away. Matthew just let her cry. A few moments passed and she leaned her head back, the lump still in her throat. Matthew smiled at her and scooped her up in his arms. They headed to the kitchen. He sat her on the countertop as she furiously wiped her tears away with the back of her hand.

"Those big ole brutes," she was getting her composure back under control." This is the nicest thing they've ever done."

Matthew was fixing coffee. Compliments of the boys, the ole cook stove was already hot so the coffee wasn't long getting ready. Cat had left the kitchen and wandered around looking everything over. He found her in the sitting room. She was standing in front of a painting that she had never seen before. The small tin plaque read. 'Howard and Eva Webb'. They looked so young.

Matthew handed her a cup of his special coffee. "Wow... who are they?"

Cat took her first sip of coffee.

"Mm mm..." she moaned "This is so good" under her breath. "I think they are my grandparents when they were younger. But... He looks a little like Uncle Joe. What do you think Matthew?"

"He does, I agree. However, except for her hair color, you are a spitting image of her."

"If you say so!" The two went hand in hand, with a cup of coffee filling their other hand. They wandered around the house exploring.

They found a very large bedroom on the ground floor. In it was the biggest bed Cat had ever seen. It had a headboard that was elegantly hand carved. The carving was of the very house they stood in. It had a tree on each side, complete with beautifully carved leaves.

Matthew plopped on the bed. "I have never laid on a bed that my feet didn't hang off of. Well, not since I was a kid." He rolled over on his back. "I've never in my life been as happy as I am now." Rolling to his side he patted the beside him and smiled at Cat. His eyes were full of passion and desire.

"Matthew Webster." Cat stared sternly. "Get your backside off that bed, there will be time for that later!"

"Ugh, woman, you're killing me." He rose and they continued to explore the old homestead.

A short time later after they'd had another cup of coffee, the two of them headed to the barn to feed their horses. When they finished, they headed for the big house.

At the long table sat six men eating fresh bread and slices of roast. Cat sat down and Daisy slid a plate in front of her, then another beside her for Matthew. Before Matthew could sit, Daisy said: "Matthew Webster, come with me to me wee kitchen." And stomped off.

"Ok, boys." Cat chirped. "What have you done to Daisy." Keith pushed a cup of coffee towards Cat. She laughed.

Uncle Joe got up and started into the kitchen. "GET OUT!" Daisy yelled at him.

The voices in the kitchen were so soft that those at the table couldn't hear their conversation. After about fifteen minutes. Daisy had a tear-streaked face that was supporting a very large smile. She filled the fresh cups and Matthew passed them to them all. She had a cup for herself. She walked up to Joe's chair and simply said. "Scoot your chair backward a wee bit, do ya hear me now?" Joe scooted his chair back without rising. His eyes were wide. Questions dance at the surface. Daisy plopped herself on his lap with her coffee in her hand. Joe's face turned red. "Drink your coffee now lads... you'll see I've won." She raised her cup like a salute and they all laughed.

The expression on Joe's face told them then, he had just died and gone to heaven. He wrapped an arm around Daisy. The coffee was wonderful.

Chapter 7

TENSIONS RISING

The next morning Cat woke up snuggled inside Matthew's arms. She opened her eyes to see the sun trying to reach the horizon. Matthew jerked the quilts off her. "Matthew" she screamed. "I'm naked!"

"I know," he said giving her a sheepish grin. She rolled onto her belly hiding her face and front side. "The view is just as pleasant as the other." Matthew laughed then flipped the quilt back over her and she snuggled into him.

Cat sat up in bed. Her cheeks were burning hot. "You my wonderful husband are wicked." They laughed, kissed, and got up, then dressed for the day.

As they walked into Daisy's kitchen, Matthew grabbed the coffee pot. Daisy elbowed Cat and nodded to Matthew. He took a sip. "Aww Daisy... You learned fast." He grinned. Cat stole his cup out of his hand. She sipped then smiled, winked at Daisy, then walked off with Matthew's cup. "Hey!" he hollered at her.

Cat slid into the chair that sat between her uncle and brother.

"Morning Colt... morning Uncle Joe." They both looked up from the papers they had been reading. She smiled and stated. "I stole Matthew's Coffee."

They all laughed. Uncle Joe picked up the papers and placed them in the pouch that the sheriff had brought.

Matthew came into the room. He sat his new cup on the table in front of Cat. Scooped her up, sat down in her chair, and set her in his lap. Picking up his cup Colt said.

"Mr. Webster." He tapped his fingers on the table. "The boys and I will be forever in your debt. Best coffee ever." He raised his cup. "Cheers," He roared.

"I heard that Laddy. Keep it up and ya may find a wee bit of hot sauce in yer eggs." Daisy replied.

Daisy came in and Uncle Joe scooped her into his lap. She blushed. It was a great start to the day.

Colt and Matthew helped Daisy in the kitchen after they had eaten. Uncle Joe and Cat were on the porch with their coffee in their hand.

"Cat, are you watching this?" Cat looked up. She noticed that the boys were working faster at their chores than she could ever remember. Uncle Joe started laughing. "The race is on baby girl, Pappy told them after they finished the chores, he was going to pick the first four finished, to take to the gate with him, to fetch Matthew's sisters. Uncle Joe chuckles bellowed. "It's going to be fun watching sixteen of them drooling over two females. Yep, kitty Cat, this will be pure entertainment."

Matthew was standing behind them watching. "Well," said Colton. "One of them is going to be upset on the get-go. Pappy already asked me to come with him. That will leave three."

A short time later with Pappy in the wagon, they headed for the gate, leading two horses.

Pappy pulled up the team at the front gate. Then turned them around to face home. He climbed down and swung wide. "Looks like we got here on time. I hear it coming up the road." Colt stood up in his stirrups. The coach slowed and came to a stop then turned in. Pappy walked over to the driver and introduced himself. "Please to meet ya, sir." The driver replied. "I have three passengers for you. Then I'm heading to Severy to drop off the last one. You got any mail going out?"

The driver was all business. "Yes sir... I got a pouch for the sheriff there in Severy." Pappy handed the pouch up to the driver. He lifted a wooden lid under his seat and dropped it in. He then turned and unbuckled the strap to release the trunks and luggage.

"All this goes with you except the small trunk here in the front."

" Did you say you had three passengers for us?" Colton asks with a surprised look on his face.

The men were loading the trunks and luggage into the wagon. "Yes sir... is there a problem?" the driver questioned.

"No sir" A woman replied. "There is no problem. "Three of us have paid to be deposited right here."

"Yes, Mam." Colton smiled and tipped his hat. "No problem at all." He extended his hand and helped her step out. "I am Colton Webb, Brother-in-law to Matthew Webster."

Shock, then humor flashed in her eyes. She smiled and took his hand. "Randy... Andrew... a little assistance please." The boys rushed forward. Next out of the coach, another lady. Randy helped her down. Andrew stepped up next. A tiny hand reached out with a tiny voice that said. "I'm still sleepy." Andrew picked up the child by her waist and carried her bride-style to the wagon. He was grinning ear to ear.

Colton turned to the ladies, "Matthew said you would rather sit a horse, it's western saddles, will that be a problem?"

"Not at all..." She smiled. "Good ole Matthew always thinking of others." The wagon was loaded. The child was seated beside Pappy. He was already talking to her. The first lady walked up to an empty saddle and mounted. It was Colton's horse.

The boys started to chuckle and Randy held out the reigns to the second one. She took the reins and mounted.

Colton turned to the driver. Pappy had his wagon already moving up the lane heading for the house. The stage driver was standing in the seat as he buckled the last trunk in place. His body lurched over the boot just as everyone had heard the shot.

The stagecoach took off... straight up the lane following the wagon. A woman still inside the coach screamed. "Tom... Andrew" Colton yelled in a panic. "Get them to the house! Randy... Loren... get that stagecoach shutdown!"

Colton jumped into the first empty saddled horse, racing for the runaway coach. The other two boys were already closing in. One on each side. They slowed the coach down and Colt climbed up in it. His horse high-tailed it up the lane heading for the house. Colton pulled the coach to a stop. Its side door flew open then out jumped another lady. Skirts flying, she did a belly flop into the dirt. Randy was off his horse and to her side in a flash. He rolled her over onto his folded knees gently. She opened her eyes in panic.

"Hold on... take it easy... are you hurt?" she shook her head.

"Hurry it up down there" Colton calmly said. "This driver is in a bad way."

"Well, sweet lady," Randy said as she was still trying to catch her breath. "Shall we get you back into the coach?"

"No," she said in a panic. "I'll take a horse." Randy looked around.

Loren was in the saddle holding Randy's mount. "Well... I guess you ride with me." Loren stepped down; Randy mounted. Loren helped the 3rd lady onto the back of Randy's horse then he swung back into the saddle. Colton was already headed to the house with the empty stagecoach, and the driver laying on top.

Seven men stood in the lane as Colton pulled the stage to a stop it took all eight to get the driver down and into the big house. Then Joe sent two riders to alert the shcriff.

After the driver was unloaded, Joe sent four of his boys to see what they could find at the sight of the attack. When they were closer to the end of the lane Bart pulled up his horse.

"Have your guns ready boys... We don't know who might still be around."

With guns ready the boys cautiously began searching. Shortly Keith called out.

"Over here, guys... Looks like we have a man down."

"We see you.... come out of the brush... you are surrounded," Loren called out. But got no reply. "Step out with your hands empty... you have four guns on you. "Again, no response.

Bart yelled out loudly "I'm coming in, your hands better be empty!" Slowly and carefully the four boys approached.

The man was laying at the edge of the brush, not moving. Hunter kicked his gun away from him. He was dead. After another search of the area, they found his horse not too far away. The boys tied his body to his horse and also discovered another horse that had been tied close by. The second horse and rider had headed east. Hunter took the horse and body they found and took off to the ranch. The other three continued to track the missing rider. After two hours had passed, the tracks were still proceeding east. The boys turned back. When Loren and the boys reached the ranch-house they reported what they had done to Joe.

Cat and Pappy and the boys unload the wagon into her house. She ushered the ladies and children inside. Colt unstrapped the last trunk off the top of the stage. Poppy took it into Cats house also. Knowing the driver was in good hands he had Randy bring the new guest and they went into Cat's new house.

As Randy stepped in with his lady rider. Matthew's sisters rushed to her side.

"Oh Lori," said the taller one.

"Are you ok..." the three hugged.

"Randy... Colt... Where's Matthew?" Cat was calmer than the other three.

"Uncle Joe has sent three riders to fetch the Doc. Matthew is taking care of all the horses. He'll be in shortly Cat. So, let's all try to get calm and we'll get this sorted out." Then Colt turned to Randy "Have Daisy fix coffee and bring some of her rolls." Randy turned to leave. "Wait... have

Loren and Pappy bring about eight chairs." Randy went out the door.

"Ladies" Cat smiled. "Let's sit for a few minutes. Introductions are in order. I am Cat Webster; Matthew and I were married yesterday." She waved her hand around "I'll explain that later."

"I am Michell, Matthew's oldest sister, but please don't call me that. I go by Missy. This is our younger sister Sara." Cat shook their hands. "This little missy is Ivy. She and her mother were left in our town. Ivy's father passed away. We took them in, Aunt Martha wouldn't have it any other way. Three months later and Ivy's mother got sick. The sickness took her a few weeks later. That was four and a half years ago. Ivy is seven now and quite the pistol. But we love her, she is our other sister."

When the door opened, Daisy walked in with coffee and cups, Randy was holding the door with cookies and rolls. They sat everything down on the table and turned to meet the new guests.

Randy handed Ivy a cookie as he squatted down to chat with her. Cat-filled cups. Daisy seemed to be distracted by Ivy and Randy. She turned to hand Sara and Missy their cups. They seemed in shock. "Sara... Missy... are you two all right?" Daisy looked over at them to introduce herself and immediately withdrew her hand. Both ladies had their mouths open.

Matthew and Uncle Joe entered the house. Little Ivy broke the silence. "Know what," she said taking Daisy's hand. Ivy pulled on Daisy's hand and she squatted down. "You look just like the picture that Sara has. It's a picture of my mommy."

Daisy smiled and asked kindly. "Now wee one, that is mighty sweet. And what might yer mummy's name be?"

"I don't remember her much... she died when I was really little... But I do know her name. She left a letter for me. Mommy's name was Rose."

Daisy's fist flew to her chest and she passed out cold. Uncle Joe carried Daisy to the sitting room and lay her on the couch. Sara brought a cool wet cloth placing it on her forehead. Joe continued to pat the back of her hand.

By the time Daisy was able to collect her thoughts, Sara, Missy, and Ivy were sitting on the low table in front of her. All three were smiling.

Ivy was twisting her pigtail. Daisy sat up slowly as Joe slid closer.

Ivy leaned close to Daisy's eyes. "Did you know I'm almost as big as Cat?" She whispered. Daisy blinked. The room filled with laughter. Ivy straightened up and carefully climbed into Daisy's lap. When she settled, she said. "Sara and Missy told me your name is Daisy. Daisies are flowers just like my mommy's name is a flower." She reached over and picked up Uncle Joe's hand and looked up. "Mister you have big hands." Joe showed her his best smile.

"Daisy" Ivy asked her, "Would you like to see a picture of my mommy?"

Daisy nodded and Ivy slipped a small piece of paper into her hand.

Daisy looked at the picture the child had just handed her. "Ivy," she said, "Did you know... your mummy was my wee baby sister?" Ivy wiggled in Daisy's arms. "I like that." Ivy giggled. When Daisy tore her eyes away from Ivy, Missy handed her an envelope. It read. "To my sister Daisy, from Rose."

Matthew, Missy, and Sara chatted, hugged, and got caught up with each other. Uncle Joe, Cat, Colt, and Randy talked about the stage-coach driver. Daisy and Ivy got to know each other a little bit.

Pappy pushed the door opened and hollered in. "Soups on." They all left to eat in the big house.

After the meal, all the women were in the kitchen cleaning up the mess and talking and laughing. Getting to know each other. Daisy was at her happiest. Having the women around seemed to be the thing she was most needing. Putting away the coffee cups Cat spied Matthew watching them. When he knew Cat had seen him, he came walking up to her.

"Matthew" Cat called out with a smile. "Are you spying on me?" He scooped her up bride-style into his arms. "I sure am babe; I haven't got to kiss you all day." Their lips touched and Ivy screamed, "Ewwwwwwww, they are kissing."

Out the door, they went with Missy and Sara following. Ivy was helping herself to her newly found Aunt Daisy's cookies. Uncle Joe got her and himself both a glass of milk. "I love it here Uncle Joe," Ivy said. "Do you think I could stay?"

Lori stood looking out the window watching the tall grass bend with the breeze. She chewed on her fingernail, lost in thoughts.

"Excuse me please" Lori looked up. "Lori, is it?" Tom waited and she nodded. "I know we haven't met yet. My name is Tom. Tom Horn." She nodded "I was wondering if you might know Bev Young. She's from outside of Severy. Lori smiled.

"Lori Jones." She extended her hand. "Bev and I have been friends for a long while." Lori's shyness showed.

"Do you know if she'll be coming to the gathering at the end of the month?"

"No, Tom... I don't know, I've been away for about a year. I received a letter from her at Christmas but..." Randy looked a little peeved.

"Randy... Lori here knows my sweetheart, they are friends. Been friends for years. If you are taking Lori back home to Severy tomorrow, I am begging you, let me go with you." Tom was pleading. Lori began to tremble, "My pa, don't know I'm coming. He's not expecting me. I... I...

I don't have anywhere to go ... Bev doesn't know I'm coming... I just wanted to see her one more time again to say goodbye. Maybe I am a stupid fool. Just like Pa always told me I was." Lori was looking at the floor tears flowing down her face. She didn't sound like she was crying, but she was.

"Randy," Tom said gently. "Pull Lori's chair out." Tom led Lori to the chair at the big table. Randy sat close beside her, Tom on the other. Joe and Daisy stood in the doorway. The boys were unaware.

Gently Tom placed his hand on Lori's back. "You are the friend Bev has told me about." Lori wouldn't look up. "Your pa used to beat you when he was drunk, lock you in the root cellar." Tom sighed. "Lori, look at me." She shook her head. Randy gently took her hand. "Bev and I are going to be married at the gathering. We won't make you go home to your pa, or anywhere near Severy." Randy squeezed her hand carefully. "Listen to me, Lori." Tom continued. "I'll talk to Joe Webb, he's a good man. I'll see if he would hire you on, maybe help Daisy in the kitchen, he won't have a man here on the place that would hurt a woman. Nor a man who would tip a bottle. Let me talk to him. Just sit here with Randy for a minute. It'll be okay."

Randy pulled her into his arms and held her. Tom stood up.

"That sounds like a good plan boys, I heard every word. Daisy would enjoy the company." Joe walked over to Lori's side. He took her chin and lifted it so she would look at him.

"Sweet child." He said, "There's not a man on the 10 that would ever call you names or lay a hand on you, nor would they allow any other man to either."

Daisy handed Lori a lace hanky. Lori wiped her tears away. Joe continued by saying. "Honey don't lower your eyes to any man, when you need your voice to be heard, you speak up. Consider this your home, your safe place. Know that if you want to stay, then you can stay. Only you should be the one to choose what you want. No one else. Think it over then let me or one of the boys know." Slapping Randy on the back Joe said. "Look after her son."

Joe almost drags poor Daisy out the back door. She pulled her hand loose from his grip

"Joe Webb... what is going on in that head of yers? You've been actin' daft all day now."

She straightened up her blouse.

"You... you Daisy." He sputtered. "One minute you're all sweet and silly, the next you're Irish Tempers a flaring. What is it that you want me to say?"

"Ole righty I'll be tellin' ya then." Daisy put her hands on her hips. "I've been here with you from before the twins were birthed, through the thick and thin I have. Helped ya get through yer grieving. Stood firm I have. One minute I think ya might be lovin' me the next I am thinking I'm invisible to ya like some sort of ghost. Ya, kiss me on my head then the next ya kiss me on the cheeks. But not once have ya kissed me on the lips, nor tellin' me ya might have a wee bit of love fer me. Ole righty Joe Webb, yer to be a say'n that ya do love me and that I could be makin' ye a bonny good wife... Hell... I'd do everthin' else for ya."

"Uncle Joe" Cat had sang out. "You best be taking care of that." Cat was grinning as she pointed to Daisy marching out through the tall grass. "No one is to be out alone, it's your orders after all ya know?" she smiled as her Uncle Joe caught up with Daisy, and the two disappeared into the tall grass together

Sara and Missy were settled into their rooms and Ivy had her room in the big house. The Doctor stayed overnight in the guest room. The stage driver was resting and recovering in another guest room. Four of the boys stood to watch for the night, with Lori being asleep in Cat and Matthew's 3rd bedroom.

Matthew stretched out on his large bed with Cat beside him. "It's been a busy day babe, I love you more each day, Goodnight." Matthew rolled to his side...........WACK

"Cat Webster, you did not just attack my back!" Matthew laughed softly.

"Yes, Mr. Webster." She pulled him back over to face her. "You my husband are not going to go to sleep yet."

"I'm not?" He played.

"No sir... you are not. I'll be needing all those kisses that I've been missing out on all day... then you will be teaching me a few more things before we fall asleep." Then Cat added. "You got that Tall Bear?" She giggled. She knew that Matthew knew, he was a goner.

Chapter 8

INFECTIOUS LOVE

Just before daybreak, Randy had stepped outside of the Bunkhouse and took a hard stretch. As he began to relax, he noticed a lump of a figure at the steps of the big house. As his eyes focused, he realized it was a woman sitting there. She was folded up with her skirt tucked around her. She had her arms holding herself. It was Lori.

Before he had realized what he was doing his feet took him right beside her and he stopped. Without even looking up she greeted him. "Good morning, Randy."

"Morning sweet lady... how'd ya know it was me?" He asked curiously.

"It's your boots, I noticed yesterday that yours are different." She replied. "Would you sit with me for a few minutes?"

"On one condition." ... Lori looked up at him with her shy smile. "Only if you move up to the top step," Randy commented. She scooted up a step and Randy sat down beside her. "These long legs that I have been blessed with wouldn't last long down there." His heart skipped a little in his chest when she giggled at him.

Lori bumped Randy's shoulder with hers and watched his face as she slid her hand on his closest knee. Randy put his arm around her and pulled her a little closer. "What's on that mind of yours, the sun isn't even up yet."

She took ahold of his arm that was around her with both her hands. She didn't want him to take it away. Lori pulled it around her a little tighter as she looked out into the darkness.

"Randy..." Her voice sounded much firmer and more normal. "As far back as I can remember, I've been afraid... of things... people... my pa... of being stupid... or weak. It crushes me down. A year ago, I ran off. A lady I knew, ... she was a preacher's widow, told me years ago that I could come to her anytime. She said 'she knew'". Lori took a breath. "That day... the last time Pa beat me. He had passed out from the whiskey so I stole his horse. It wasn't even saddled, I put the bridle on him climbed on the corral fence, and found my way to Coffeeville."

Randy pulled her out of his arms and Lori looked up at him. He took her hands in his.

"How did that make you feel Lori?" She looked at the concern on his face, then back out into the darkness.

"At first, I was terrified he would wake up and chase me down. But my heart just kept me pushing on. A preacher said one time 'If you seek God, you will find him.' He had said that God loved me. Those words kept looping over and over in my head."

Lori leaned back against Randy's chest. "You are so warm." He snuggled her and placed his chin on top of her head. "I'm tired of being weak... of being afraid... of feeling... worthless." She took a deep breath and then let it out slowly. "Would you... or maybe Miss Cat... teach me how to be strong. Teach me to defend myself... and stuff like that? I just don't ever want a beating or bruises from any man's hands ever again."

"Oh, sweet lady," Randy said. "I could try to bribe you right now." Randy began to laugh as he hugged her. His body shook as he did. Then he straightened himself up with a serious note answered. "Yes... yes, I will and I'm sure Miss Cat will help."

Lori pulled away and stood up. Smiling, she put her hand on her hip. "And what is this bribe you are thinking?"

Randy stood and walked over to her keeping her at arms-length The sun was just peeking over the horizon. He put his hands on her shoulders. Lori could see the sunlight making his eyes sparkle.

"The bribe would be..." He hesitated. "I'll only do this for you if you will be my girl."

It was the first time that Randy had seen a real smile on Lori's face. "I'll accept that bribe." She spoke. "Looks like this is my first win." Then she smiled again as a light blush touched her cheeks.

A jolly voice spoke out from the door of the big house. "Ok, Lord... I hear you, looks like I'll be needing to build a few more houses." It was Joe Webb. "By the way kids... coffee is ready."

Randy scooped Lori up bridal style, looked her in the eyes, and asked. "Are you ready for this?"

"Yes!" she hollered and laughed genuinely for what she could recall as the first time.

With breakfast over all the ladies and Ivy ran the men out of the kitchen. Daisy was at her happiest. The fuss, laughter, and chatter were the best things Joe had witnessed in a long time.

"Several riders coming in," Randy reported. "I've alerted the boys." Then he added. "Matthew and Tom are headed out to check on the boys riding the herd."

Joe nodded "Coffee's on the stove" He put on his gun belt and went out the door.

Randy stopped at the kitchen door. "Is it safe for me to enter this hens meeting?" Cat whacked him in the chest and Sara threw a towel at him. They all laughed. Someone said. "Only if you're brave enough". Lori picked up a cup, filled it, and handed it to Randy. He winked at her.

"So, Randy" Lori plucked a piece of hay off his vest. "Now that I am your girl, what am I supposed to be doing?" The ladies burst into fits of laughter waiting for his answer.

Reaching down he placed a light, slightly lingering a kiss on her lips. "Looks to me, sweet girl... You've already figured it out."

"By the way ladies." Randy's serious tone brought all eyes up." We've got riders coming in from the gate.

"I'll get me a coffee going." Barked Daisy.

"I'll get a tray of cups." Missy chimed in.

"I'll grab cream and sugar," Lori added

"Looks like I'll help set the table." Cat laughed.

Three Pinkerton men, three stagecoach men, Sheriff Steve, and a woman, and a man, were dismounting as the ladies stepped out of the big house. With Cat in the lead, they all were heading for Joe. Cat checked to see if her thong was off her pistol.

"Good morning, Joe" Sheriff Steve smiled. "This is quite the reception." Starting with the Pinkerton men Steve began the introductions. He then motioned to the stagecoach company men. Then to the man and woman. The lady was untying a rather large bundle from behind her saddle. "And this is Kirk Young and his daughter Bev."

Everyone knew Bev by name only. But they knew her. Randy led Lori up behind Bev. "Let me give you a hand with that," Randy said. Bev turned around. There before her, stood her long-lost friend.

The reunion was more than either of them had expected. After the hugging and screaming and a little more hugging the girls walked away arm in arm.

Mr. Young turned to the sheriff. "You tell me you ain't gonna arrest her Steve. That was Lori Cain. The one that stole her pa's horse about a year back."

"If I'd have known her back then, I'd have saddled it for her." The Sheriff grinned.

Joe held up both hands. "Just hang for a few minutes on men." He turned and motioned to all in the yard. "Let's take this to the house, the coffee is ready."

"Loren" Joe shouted "You stand watch, the rest of you come on in. Send Tom and Matthew in soon as they are back."

"I can see them now." Bart called out, he was standing in the loft "Give them about five minutes."

The crowd of the mixed company headed to the big house. The ladies were filling cups, cream, and sugar in the center of the table. "Let's get started". It was one of the Pinkerton men.

"We sir do not work like that!" Cat barked at him. She was up in his face before he knew where she had even come from "Every man, woman, and child on The 10 are involved one way or another. AND" he knew by the tone of her voice, and the venom in her eyes that he was going to stand down. "There's no reason to have to repeat this conversation, so do not bark orders to anyone in my home, you got that sir?"

"I do... I beg your pardon." With that, he took a seat.

"Colt... is the pouch still inside on the stage-coach?" Randy spoke.

"It is... I'll fetch it." Colt headed out the door. "Bart come with me!" he added "Uncle Joe's orders." Colt grinned.

"Let's all get seated," Cat said. "Ladies you too, this is how things work around here."

Lori sat down with Bev beside her. Randy walked over to her, scooped Lori up, and sat her down on his lap. He kissed her cheek and mumbled. "Just making sure there are enough chairs to go around." And then smiled at her.

Colt, Bart, Matthew, and Tom all came through the door one after the other. Mr. Young stood up and walked to Tom. "Tom" Mr. Young shook his hand "Good to see you"

"Mr. Young" Tom took his handshake. "Is this called business or pleasure?"

"That's what I like about you son." He laughed "Right to the point." He stepped sideways and swooped his arm like a bow, a motion for Tom to step forward. Instantly his eyes found Bev's. For Tom, there was no one else in the room.

Joe Webb stood up "Yep.... God has already let me know that we will be building more houses here on the 10."

Everyone laughed. "Tom, you and Bev have some catching up to do"

Cat charged. "So, if it's all right with Uncle Joe, why don't you and Bev get your coffee and head for the porch? You aren't gonna hear one word of this anyway." Everyone chuckled and Joe pointed the couple out of the room. With that, Cat sat down in her husband's lap and stated thusly. "All right ladies and gentlemen, let us begin now." She nodded to the Pinkerton man.

"I must say Mrs. Webster" He began. "It's wonderful to know that there are women out here that know how to speak their mind while remaining a lady. Also knowing how to handle herself as well as protect themselves." He nods towards her pistol and gun belt. "If more men were open to this, life would be so much better for everyone." He continued; his eyes looked over all that was in this room. "Women who have to hide away in holes, attics, and under beds trembling when caught out here on their own... they suffer things that they shouldn't have to...or are killed... and worse. I praise your men for understanding this." The room was silent.

"Now then, I believe... Colt, is it?... has a pouch for me?" Colton handed the pouch over to him and he finished with. "I do hope you have accepted my apology as it was sincere. Now I think I'll have another cup of that coffee while my partners discuss the reason we are here."

The Tully company had finally been taken down. One of their top men had been critically wounded and was still in a hospital in Joplin town, his name is Wes Price. Recovering he was still under guard. The man agreed to turn over documents to help take this company down. He admitted that he couldn't stomach how violent it had become. He had been a friend and an employee of its original owner. This man also wanted to return money and land deeds to their rightful owners.

The Body of the individual found the other day from the stagecoach shootout was Identified as Dan Connor, and is a cousin to Pete Connor. So even though the Tully company is going under, it's safe to say that Pete Connor is still out there, and probably looking to cause trouble. So do be mindful, with the majority of the company gone however I do believe this is something to celebrate!

Because this was his idea, the judge and the Pinkerton who had humbly apologized to Cat said. "I think that this calls for a celebration maybe you have some scotch?"

Joe looked to Cat and nodded "Sir... from the day this land was claimed, The 10" she said. "There have not been any alcoholic beverages allowed. It is our own 'Law'. We celebrate with fun, games, food, and love... will fresh coffee do?"

"That it will, I have been far and wide over a lot of lands and haven't had coffee this good." Matthew and Daisy beamed.

The last, the third Pinkerton cleared his throat. He had everyone's attention. "We do have one last matter to cover."

Everyone quieted down and he picked up the pouch. Holding it up with one hand he then sat it down back on the table top with a thud. "This has to do with you, Mrs. Webster." Matthew's cuddling hold changed into a firm embrace. "It seems that the man you describe as a 'fowl pig' has escaped us... I read that you bashed his face in with your gun butt."

"His name we've learned is 'Pete Conner'. I've never tracked a man as evil and vile as he is. Three women were shot to death because he didn't like them, another he beat to death with his hands." Lori was trembling in Randy's arms.

"From the time he had his run-in with you Mrs. Webster... up to date, he makes it known he won't stop until he has you dead in your tracks."

The only sound was a bird chirping outside. "Matthew... you are crushing the air out of me." Cat struggled.

Joe cut in "Do you have any advice or plans we should attempt..."

Sheriff Steve spoke, "Keep your folk ready... aware... alert... no one rides alone." He continued. "Your plans so far are working." All three Pinkertons nodded.

The stagecoach men ate lunch and visited with the boys, then collected their horses. After they hooked the coach to the team, they headed out of the lane. The wounded driver remained. Doc said he could travel at the end of the next week.

Chapter 9

STRONGER TOGETHER

*T*wo Days Till the Gathering.

Matthew was sitting at the head of the table, Cat in his lap. Tom and Bev are in another chair. Missy, Sara, Daisy, and Lori were also seated at the table. Randy approached Cat, pulling Lori to his side. Randy dropped to one knee before Cat. Lori then said, "Randy, shouldn't you ask Matthew first?"

"No sweet lady," He said lovingly, "It's not like that here on The 10. Matthew will add his opinion and most likely his help." He turned to Lori and stood "The men on The 10 don't silence our ladies. We don't make them ask permission, or cower in a corner." He tipped her chin up so she would look into his eyes. "We... all the men on The 10 know how important it is for our women to share their opinions, their thought, all the things they want with everything they want. This sweet lady is part of what you want and need to learn about."

Sara and Daisy were blinking back their tears. Randy turned to Cat who was still in Matthew's lap grinning "If you weren't so dad-blamed tall you wouldn't have to get on your knee." Cat's smiling smirk was all over her face.

"And if you weren't so dad-blamed short little kitty Cat the rest of us wouldn't have to." Laughter filled the room. Lori's eyes were wide. She smiled. "Now Cat... I and Lori were thinking... and she wants to learn how to defend herself, fight so to speak, shoot a pistol, watch out for dangers, and such. All these ladies should too." His hand waved around to the others. "Do ya think you could help Lori out a little? And anyone else that wants the same thing."

"I'm in for it," Cat said, then every man and woman in the room joined in as well.

"Sounds like a plan," Joe sang out. "But everyone keeps in mind that the gathering is in two days, and a lot of work needs done."

Colt, Matthew, Tom, Randy, and Garret worked with the girls for just over an hour. Cat was top-notch, Missy was very good, and Sara was pretty fair. Lori and Bev were new to all of it but were great students.

Then five girls and five boys as Cat still called them headed to the barn, The work began. Preparing for the gathering they cleaned out the dust, hay, and cobwebs. The stalls were mucked and no horses were allowed inside again until the gathering was over.

Tables and benches were brought down from the loft using ropes and pulleys. Everyone had a good time talking and pulling pranks while getting the work done.

Joe whistled out later in the afternoon and everyone headed into cleanup.

Missy and Matthew noticed looking especially nice that evening as fourteen bodies sat down to eat at a table made for twelve. Colt sat beside her. Cat shot a glance at her husband as if to say "Did I miss something?" Matthew squeezed her hand, leaned in, and whispered. "Shhhh, don't say anything." Then kissed her.

After the meal was cleaned up, four couples were standing in the yard talking about today's activities. Garret, Joe, Pappy, and Daisy were on the porch. Ivy was in Pappy's lap.

Tom and Bev were laughing about Matthew and Cat's story of their surprise wedding. Missy asked, "You mean you didn't get to dance after?" She played like she was having a panic attack. The laughter continued.

Daisy swatted Pappy "Why hadn't we been a thinkin' on this?" Her Irish charm was having fun. "Pappy... off ye go... get yer fiddle and play the newlyweds a wee bit of a jig"

Pappy returned with his instrument and began to play some very lively tunes. Lori was the only one who didn't know how to dance. She ended up with more teachers than she needed. It had been a good day.

Chapter 10

WEIGHT OF THE PAST

One Day Before the Gathering

The next morning after breakfast was cleared eleven people sat at the table going over what was left to do for the gathering on the next day. Cat topped off everyone's cup and set the coffee pot back down. Matthew had stepped into the kitchen with her. "Mr. Webster" She smiled. "With everything and everyone working yesterday, you shorted me on kisses."

Matthew closed the distance between them. "Well babe, I guess I will have to double up on them today" He scooped her up and took her out the door. Cat laughing all the way. Each couple giggled and looked at each other.

"Y'know what m'lady" Colt said to Missy. "That brother of yours is full of good ideas" He stooped and kissed Missy. It was their first kiss.

"Yep," Joe said to no one in particular. "I see that another house is going to go up on The 10."

Off to the back of the barn but mostly to the side, wooden slats made a ladder. It led up the side of the big tree. In that tree was a platform of barn wood. It had four sides around it, three feet high, and a trap door on the floor. A few days earlier Joe had taken Ivy there and showed it to her. The two had checked it out to be sure it was still sturdy and solid. Ivy loved it. It would be her fort, Joe told her she could be the boss of it. Joe and Ivy had just finished sprucing up.

"It's the nicest thing, Uncle Joe!" She had told him. "You are the best….. like a daddy. I never had a daddy I could remember." He told her when the children came to the gathering only four could go up there at a time. She agreed.

The work was finished everything was ready. Now they could all relax.

After the evening meal, everyone sitting at the big table began to reminisce about the gatherings that had come and gone, and about friends and neighbors who were still around. And those who had passed. Lori, Matthew, Missy, and Sara enjoyed the stories but had never been to one.

"Cat and I had planned to get married there." Matthew laughed. "But Washee had different plans for us," he said.

Daisy piped in "Yep, Laddy, and ever since that happened, yer a been dripping love all over me floors."

The rafters rang out in laughter. Matthew blushed.

"Will you look at that?" Colton hollered. "The man is blushing."

When the laughing had finally died down Joe spoke up. "Alrighty then." He swallowed hard. "I'm thinking, if Daisy will have me, I'd like to be in that wedding line, right behind Bev and Tom." Joe was on one knee before Daisy and held out a tiny silver band.

"Aw shoot. Ya big clod." She brushed a tear away and sniffled. "I thought you'd never be askin' me, ya know I will."

Matthew kicked Colt under the table. "Ouch! Dang Matthew! Give me a minute will you." Colton stood up and limped a little.

Matthew gave Colton a devilish grin.

"Well dang Colt, you asked me two days ago for my blessing. "Matthew was laughing. Cat buried her head in his chest. "What the heck is taking you so long." Matthew followed with "Well, well, would you look at that, he's blushing like a girl," Everyone was doubled over howling. Everyone except Colt and Missy.

"Yes" was all Missy said before Colt could even ask.

"I was told, that I could speak whenever I wanted to" Everyone looked at Lori. She was standing beside Randy. "Is this true?" She was looking at Cat.

"Yes, honey." Cat held her gaze, she knew how hard this was for Lori. "Whatever you want to say, anything... go ahead just speak up." Lori's eyes glanced to the floor. "No, no sweety... Don't bow your head down. You lift that chin high. You are a member of the 10, we stand straight up and tall."

Lori swallowed and straightened her posture. "I... I..." She took another deep breath and let it out slowly. Randy took her hand. "I have fallen in love with Randy and want to know how long should I have to wait until I marry him."

Her eyes never left Cats eyes. Cat smiled carefully and cocked her head to one side, then shifted her eyes to Randy, Questions danced through Cat's eyes.

Randy pulled Lori around to face him. "If you think that you are ready for marriage, if this is really what you want to do..." Randy paused for only a second. " I know I'm ready. Then you only have to wait until tomorrow."

"Tomorrow it is then." Lori kissed him and Randy folded her into his arms.

"Yep, Daisy." Joe Snickered. "Add one more house to that list!"

Matthew woke up and rolled over. Using what was left of the moonlight to check his pocket watch again. Fifteen minutes until the five o'clock hour. He rolled over and snuggled Cats back against his chest. Settling on the pillow with his chin on top of her head she sighed. Cat reached up and patted his cheek.

"Is it time to get up and get started?" she questioned.

"In a minute," Matthew told her. "Babe... all the things you have done for Lori, made me so proud of you." He sighed. "I never told you, but a long time ago, before I met up and joined Colt, to be a scout, a young Amish girl... She was maybe fourteen-fifteen years old. Had been stolen from her people. The town was in a panic." Matthew got out of bed and walked to the basin and poured himself a glass of water. He took a long cool drink and sat the glass down.

"Don't stop there Matthew." Cat encouraged him to continue. "It seems this is hard for you to speak about."

"It is... just as hard as it was for Lori to ask Randy to marry her" Matthew sat down on the side of the bed. "Anyway" he continued. "Everyone close by was out looking for her. I tracked a set of tracks; it was of a horse carrying a big load. I found her Cat."

Cat got up and gathered Matthews and her clothes. She handed him his clothes. "Go on sweetheart, just keep going. Whatever it is... just let it go... let it out."

Matthew started putting his shirt on. "She was huddled up in a ball, naked.... nothing but fear in her eyes. She was shaking with cold. Her teeth were chattering.... when she saw me.... I put a finger to my lips so she wouldn't say anything... or move."

Cat was already dressed. She was looking at Matthew. Her heart was breaking. Matthew looked like he was in a trance remembering this horrible scene. Cat handed him his long johns.

Matthew took them and began pulling them on. "I picked up a stick of firewood Cat. When that beast of a man took a pull of his jug. I busted him in the face." Matthew's eyes were facing the window but Cat was sure he wasn't staring at anything in particular.

She handed him his clean socks. "I knocked him out cold Cat. I grabbed that child's clothes and took them to her. She flinched away from me. I spoke to her soft like and slowly started to gain some trust. I practically had to dress her myself. Moving her closer to the fire she began to find trust in me."

Cat handed Matthew his pants. "Cat, ... she had bruises all over her body. When I finally got her settled. I thought about that man who had done this and I went to make sure he was still out. I was 16 years old Cat... I had killed him with my bare hands."

It was then that Cat went to his side and held Matthew. "I made sure the girl could see the town and watched to be sure she made it."

Pulling out of his arms she handed him his boots. "What happened next Matthew."

"I ran Cat, ... I was sixteen.... just killed a man.... and helped a child who had been raped and beaten, back to safety. I've told no one Cat. Just you, just now. When Lori was afraid that we would take her to her father's place.... the fear in her eyes was the same fear that was in the eyes of that Amish child. It made this ghost I've carried surface again."

"Matthew, look at me." Cat got his attention. "Think about this just for a minute. Washee told you that you carried a burden. That it was not yours to carry. She told you that the Great Spirit gave you a task. That you completed that task. That it was for you to do. That no more would suffer because of a beast. That you were to let go of that burden. I heard her words but had no idea what she was talking about. Washee knew Matthew. She is that close to the Great Spirit."

Cat continued. "You spoke about this out loud Matthew.... your words were to me.... to tell me this story. But as you spoke this story, you were releasing this. It's not hiding inside you anymore. It's over now. You did what you had to do at that time. Now you have to set that burden down. Now you Matthew Webster, can walk away from it. You don't have to carry it any longer."

Cat sighed. "You are a wonder man. I love you so much. We are as Washee says. We have become one." She held Matthew until he finally relaxed. "Are you ready?" Cat asked. "I need some of your coffee."

"Hey," Matthew stated. "It wasn't me that you fell in love with, it was my coffee, wasn't it?"

"I'll never admit to that sweetheart." He threw her on the bed and tickled her until she screamed with giggles and woke up the entire house.

Chapter 11

Gathering Day

Wagons and riders started pulling in around eight o'clock that morning. Everything was set up. Ladies were fussing with the food things and children ran playing and screaming. Men sat and stood in groups talking. Horses lined the corals and hitching posts.

Everyone had their duties to finish before everyone from the community arrived. Six men rode out for a quick check on the cattle two headed North, two South, Two East, and Two West. All the other hands remained to finish up around the homestead.

Hunter and Loren rode west. They had the most territory to cover. As they began the ride back to the homestead, Loren noticed a horse without a rider beside the lake. This horse was very unfamiliar to them.

Hunter stated. "Maybe someone coming today has had a fall. Let's go check it out."

"Just be on the lookout... We've had some unwelcomed guests around." Loren replied.

The men scouted around and approached with caution. When they didn't see any danger, they approached the horse and dismounted.

"Hunter.... this looks like a dry camp." Loren sighed, still feeling on edge. "This is a young horse, and its reigns are busted." The horse was nervous and wasn't sure if it could trust the men. After speaking to it gently and quietly they were able to approach it in a rather safe manner.

"Looks like someone tied it up and he didn't like it." Hunter chuckled.

"Maybe so... but I'm not liking this... Whoever the rider was, was here overnight if not longer. This doesn't feel right." Loren stated as he was scanning the area for a man. "You can see the back of the barn from here." He squatted down and looked at the tracks.

"Hunter over here!" Loren pointed out the empty whiskey bottle sitting near the clump of tall grass.

"We need to get on back and let Joe and Matthew know. The sheriff may already be here."

The boys mounted up and led the riderless horse with them. Picking up the pace they headed for the ranch house. Both were having uneasy feelings grow inside them.

Matthew stood watching Keoto. He was helping Washee down the trail. As he looked down, he saw a small flat white stone it was oval. Picking it up he could see it had a hold through the edge of it. Turning he went into the barn and took a leather string and ran it through the hole in the stone. With the ends tied closed he walked up the trail to greet Keoto and Washee.

"Tall Bear" Washee spoke. "It is a fine day for a gathering."

"I have pouches to tend to Tall Bear." Keoto was speaking. "You need to bring Washee to a chair." And off he went, leaving Matthew to ten to Washee.

"Tall bear," Washee said again. "My legs are tired." She waved her hand around the air. "Carry me to a chair." She ordered. "We will get there faster."

Matthew roared out a laugh. "I will do that, but first I have a gift for you." He showed her the stone on the string. "It is a gift to thank you for showing me how to put down the burden that I wasn't supposed to carry. I want to tell you that, and the burden showed me how to be a good person. Do you understand?"

She smiled and patted the back of his hand. "I do, now take me... over there." Matthew did as she asked.

By noon they figured everyone was there. They ate, then men and women both cleaned away the food and helped with the dishes. Daisy stood by Joe in the lane out front of the house. Beside them was a table with a piece of paper held down with a rock so the wind wouldn't blow it away. Also, a cup with a broken handle held short sharpened pencils.

Daisy held up a cowbell and rang it for Joe until all was quiet. Then Joe spoke. "it's great to see everyone gathered up today. Now let's get started sorting out the cattle drive. Who would like to speak?

No one spoke up. "How about a vote then? Mr. Young and his boys ram-rodded it last year and they did a fine job. We only lost one head." All was quiet. "Ok, then are you willing to Ramrod again Mr. Young?" Mr. Young stood up and nodded. "For those of you in the front, he said yes." Joe shifted his feet. "Does anyone object?" Silence. "All in favor for the Youngs to run the drive this say yes"

Yes, roars out over the tall grasslands.

"Now everyone knows how this is done, so come forward. Mr. Young and one of his sons are on this side. Colt and I will take the other side. Don't worry if you can't read or write, the four of us will write your headcount down and put your name with it. Those that can will, write it themselves. Let's get started we have a wedding and dancing when we are done. All the trade tables are by the barn if the ladies want to get started with that."

Four lines formed, the ladies headed to the trade tables, and all the kids were running and playing.

Cat was standing behind Matthew's chair. She wrapped her arms around him from behind. "So, what do you think Mr. Webster, of your first gathering?"

"I feel like I fit right in. Can't remember ever feeling more at home."

"I'm headed to the barn Matthew. The men are going to play horseshoes in a little bit. I need to be fetching the shoes out." Cat told him.

Matthew responded with "I'll be right behind you in a minute babe." Matthew said "I'm watching how they do this. Those shoes are heavy."

Cat could see some of the boys riding in a short distance out leading a riderless horse. Letting the moment unphased her as she was distracted by the task at hand.

Cat headed for the barn. She wove in and out of the ladies around the trade tables.

About five minutes later Keota ran full sprint up to the table, yelling "Mr. Joe, Colt..."

Wide-eyed he was gasping for air. "Miss Cats in the barn and a man is hurting her bad!"

The table turned over as the men all jumped up and ran Matthew was already halfway there. As he tuned into the barn, his pace never slowed. The man never looked up even.

Pete Conner sat straddling Cat's stomach. Slapping her hard with the back of his hand. Matthew picked him up and flung him against the barn wall. Pete slid down the wall in a heap. Matthew began to beat him. Pete had already lost consciousness and reeked of whiskey.

It took Randy, Colt, one of the boys, and the sheriff to drag Matthew off him. Uncle Joe was at Cat's side.

"Matthew, Matthew." Cat was crying out, "You're gonna kill him."

Matthew finally regained himself and picked Cat up out of the dirt.

The Sheriff hog-tied Pete, then the boys put him a little too roughly into the wagon. Two men volunteer to help make sure the sheriff got him back to jail.

Cat fell limp in Matthew's arms. Colton helped him get her in the house. The Doc was in step right behind them. He ordered Matthew out of the room so he could check her thoroughly. Colt had to practically drag him out. Missy stayed with her and that seemed to comfort Matthew a little.

Colton sat down in the closest chair to the door. Matthew paced the floor.

Sara came out of the kitchen with a wet towel. She offered it to Matthew, he shook his head and paced away.

"Matthew Webster, you better look at me," Sara yelled firmly at her brother. Matthew turned to her and her face softened. "You have dust and dirt over your face, and... tear streaks making a muddy trail right through it all... not to mention bloody knuckles.... now clean yourself up, and calm down.

Colt chuckled. "Cat's not dying in there. She didn't deserve what she got, but she's gonna be fine. Think about it, Matthew. Cat's likely to be madder than a wet hen, because a man hit her."

"You are right Colt," Matthew told him. "It's just... I didn't go with her. I'm just blaming myself."

The bedroom door opened. Missy was standing inside it not saying a word. Matthew started towards her.

Smiling she blocks Matthew from going in to be by Cat's side. She had her hand in the middle of his chest. Peeking around her brother she motioned for Colt. Missy stood up on her toes and looked her brother square in the eye. She felt Colt take her free hand. Then she said. "Oh... big brother of mine... this is partly your fault." She smiled and let Matthew pass. Colt was dragged in behind them.

Cat was laying in their big bed. Other than red cheeks and looking a little pale, she still looked fine. No black eyes, and a small bruise on one side of her cheek. Matthew fell to his knees beside her. Relief flooded his soul. Pulling her hands up to his lips he finally found his voice. "Thank the good Lord... Thank the Great Spirit... that you are okay."

Looking into his eyes, Cat studied him for a minute. The room was quiet. Tears began to flow rolling down her face.

"Cat..." Matthew said.

"Shush" she whispered. Matthew was still looking at her. "You big brute... you've done went and got me pregnant."

"She's just fine," Doc stated. "Getting back to the gathering will do her good." Out the door, he went.

"Mr. Webster... you are going to double up with them kisses from now on." Cat laughed as Matthew swooped her up and carried her out to the gathering. Seven couples were wed that day. The final plans for the cattle drive were completed, and the day ended with more good memories for all who had gathered.

All of the following week was all hands on deck as the calves were cut from the herd and taken to the holding pens.

The men from all over the county readied their herds as well. Volunteers signed up to go with the herd at last. One from each ranch. The

10 was sending four. Mr. Young and his oldest son were voted in as the ramrods.

Uncle Joe ordered lumber and at the NE and SW, two of the homes were ready to start going up.

Just outside the gate of The 10 a new house was built with a church next to it. That same year a mercantile and a blacksmith barn was established. The town of Howard Kansas took root. In the year of 1861, Kansas became a state. Howard Kansas became a town in 1870, then it was incorporated in the year 1877.

The beauty of the flint hills and Howard Kansas still exists today.